A *Mate* FOR THE *Christmas* DRAGON

A Mate for the Christmas Dragon

ZOE CHANT

I

JASPER

DECEMBER 20

FIVE DAYS UNTIL CHRISTMAS

Jasper thudded into the snowbank, arms upraised to defend himself from the vicious assault.

"Raar! Raaaaar!" his nephew roared, leaping onto his chest. Jasper lowered his arms— just in time to see that Cole hadn't jumped up empty-handed. A snowball the size of a football exploded on his face.

"Cole, leave your uncle alone!"

Jasper sat up, spitting snow, at the sound of his older sister Opal's exasperated but loving voice. He rubbed snow out of his eyes and grinned at her. Jasper had just arrived in town, spat out of the inter-city bus with a swarm of excited Christmas vacationers. He'd caught sight of Opal and his nephew across the road, loaded down with

Christmas shopping— and hadn't even had a chance to say hello before Cole launched his attack.

It was a year since he'd seen Opal last, but she hadn't changed a bit. Still the same dusting of freckles on her long Heartwell nose, the same bright eyes the color of the gem she was named after— and the same pleased-but-hiding-it scowl, which he was sure she saved just for him. He could just imagine how she would flick her wings at him if she was in her dragon form.

Jasper waved at his sister as Cole tried to stuff more snow down his collar. "Hey, sis. Not even an hour back in town and I'm attacked— argh, and frozen to death— by my own blood. What sort of a welcome do you call this?"

Opal rolled her eyes at him. He got the feeling if she hadn't been laden down with shopping bags, she would have crossed her arms.

"Maybe the sort of welcome a good-for-nothin' brother gets when he doesn't even tell his family he'll be home for Christmas? Where's your car? What did you do, bus here with the rest of the tourists?" Her jewel-toned eyes flicked from side to side, and Jasper's heart sank. He knew what she was looking for. "Oh. It's... just you, then?" she asked, her voice smaller.

"Yeah." Jasper didn't want to see the look in her eyes as he admitted it. He stood up, slinging Cole over his shoulder. The little boy whooped with excitement. "Just me— and a suitcase full of presents! What do you think, buddy? Can your old uncle Jasper come stay for Christmas?"

"Yeah! Presents!" Cole jiggled happily on Jasper's shoulder, then tugged on his ear. Jasper turned his head obediently to catch the boy's whisper. "Can we go flying, too?"

Jasper stared into his nephew's innocent, blue-black eyes. Inside him, his dragon shivered, but he couldn't let his feelings show. Not in front of Cole. He grinned, and winked at him. "Go flying? You betcha, buddy."

Opal sucked in a breath. Jasper didn't blame her. Right now, she would be wondering whether, in a few days' time, he'd ever be able to fly again.

He sighed. Whatever grim suspicions she was harboring, she was right to be worried. And she deserved more than him pretending everything was okay.

Jasper grabbed the handle of the suitcase he'd dropped when Cole launched his attack, and trundled over to his sister. She glared up at him, but her frown didn't hide the tears in her eyes.

Guilt lanced through him, double-edged: one for his human side, and one for his dragon. And a hell of a lot for his sister.

"Hey," he said softly, putting one arm around her. She elbowed him grumpily, but didn't pull away. "It's all right."

"No, it's not," Opal grumbled. "You're turning twenty-five this Christmas, and if you've come here alone, that means— you're going to have to choose..." Her shoulders slumped and she glanced up at Cole, who was busy making airplane noises and stealing Jasper's hat. *And whatever you choose, I lose part of my brother.*

Jasper's smile cracked, and he pulled his sister into a bear hug. "Hey, it's all right. I'll still be here." *Some of me, at least. Oh, hell. What am I doing to myself? To my family?*

"What's wrong?"

Jasper winced. He shouldn't have said that out loud. Now Cole was leaning over his shoulder, peering into both adults' faces.

"Are you in trouble, uncle Jasper? Mommy, is he in trouble?"

Jasper watched his sister take a deep breath and force a smile on her face. "Oh, he sure is! *So* much trouble. And you know what people get for Christmas when they've been bad, right?"

A grin cracked across Cole's face and he threw his head back with a mad cackle. "Me!"

"That's right! You get Cole in your stocking!"

Jasper stifled a snort-laugh. *You realize that joke's going to get old fast, right?*

Going to get old? It's been the number one, top Heartwell Family joke since September. It's so old, it's got wrinkles. You have a bit of catching up to do, little bro.

She smiled at him, but her eyes were still sad. Jasper's chest hurt and inside him, his dragon shivered again. Harder this time, like it wanted to shake loose from him.

He didn't blame it. Whatever happened this Christmas, one of them would end up... gone.

"Can uncle Jasper come with us to the big tree and and and you can have a coffee and I can have a cookie?" Cole implored, hanging sideways off Jasper's shoulder so he could stare imploringly at his mother. "Pleaaaaase?"

Opal snorted and flicked his nose. "I can have a coffee, huh? You sure know the way to your mommy's heart. Okay. Jas, you want to dump your stuff in the car and we can head down to the square?"

After a bit of load-swapping, where Jasper made sure he was carrying all of Opal's shopping bags, and his suitcase, and his firecracker nephew, and his sister didn't have to carry anything, Opal led the way back to the car. It was already laden down with a day's shopping, but Jasper managed to wedge his suitcase into the trunk.

His mouth watered as he peeked into a canvas bag full of holiday groceries. "You planning to feed an army, sis?"

Opal snorted. "A four-year-old dragon shifter, which is basically the same thing. You remember how much we ate at his age?"

"And more every year after..." Jasper cracked open the lid of a chiller box. "He's only going to get bigger— ooh, leg of lamb? My favorite!"

Opal slapped his hand away. "You mean, *my* favorite. I didn't even know you were coming, remember?" She shut the trunk with a thud and shot him a sideways glance. "And, not gonna lie to you, bro, I kind of wish you weren't here. You still have—" Her voice broke, but she pushed through, scowling at the car. "You still have five days—"

"For what?" Jasper checked that Cole was still distracted by the display in a nearby shop window, and stepped closer to Opal.

She narrowed her eyes. "You *know* what."

"Opal, I've spent the last five *years* traveling the world, trying to find her. If she even exists." Jasper pulled his woolen hat off and ran his fingers through his dark hair. "I've tried matchmaking services, blind dates, double dates, online dating, everything I could think of, in hundreds of cities, and I'm— I'm tired, sis. I just want to spend Christmas with my family."

Opal's eyes softened. "You know we're always here for you." She squeezed his arm. "Whatever happens."

"Thanks, sis. Now, let's go get that coffee. I think I'm going to need one, too." He grinned at her. His face felt stiff, but— he'd made his choice. And it was the right one. Wasn't it?

I want to spend Christmas with my family. Even if it's my last Christmas as myself.

Opal called Cole back over and Jasper braced himself as the little boy tackled him. He swung his nephew up on his shoulders again. Cole made his hands into claws and roared.

"Hey," Opal whispered. "Remember what we said about being a human while we're in town?"

Cole flopped forward, his arms dangling limply over Jasper's face. "Ye-es," he admitted reluctantly. When Opal looked away, he made little claws and scrabbled at Jasper's forehead. *Raar!* he roared telepathically.

I heard that, Cole Jasper Heartwell! his mother called back. "Come on. Let's go get that coffee. And your cookie, *if* you behave."

Jasper chuckled. *God, it's good to be home.* He came back to the mountains as often as he could, but with his quest to find a mate taking up most of his time for the last few years, that hadn't been much. Now that he was here, with the sky stretching endlessly overhead, and the peaks and valleys of the mountains promising hundreds of hours of fun adventures with his nephew…

Maybe it won't be so hard.

Inside him, Jasper's dragon curled into a tighter ball. Lately it had been doing that a lot. That, and shivering. Like it couldn't decide whether it wanted to hold on, or flee.

He lowered his head and followed his sister down the street.

The town square was just as he remembered it from the last Christmas he'd spent in town. A giant tree stood in the centre, festooned with gold decorations and glowing with a thousand lights. More ropes of lights were strung out from the top of the tree, connecting to the shopfronts that ran around the edge of the square, and right on top of it was a massive star that twinkled in the lights that seemed to hang in the air below it. It was magical.

Which was silly for a dragon to think, but Jasper had always had a special place in his heart for all the trappings of Christmas. It was his birthday, after all. And a time when people came together in happiness and joy, and all good things. The perfect time of year. Especially these last few years. With his quest to find his mate being such a failure, Christmases at home with his family had been the one certainty in life he could rely on.

Some of the tension in Jasper's chest unwound. He caught up with Opal in a few long strides and linked arms with her. "Where this coffee? My shout."

"There— see the piles of exhausted parents under the tree?" Opal pointed.

Low benches and chairs were arranged around glowing braziers beneath the spreading branches of the massive Christmas tree. A coffee cart designed to look like Santa's sleigh was parked in the middle of them, holding baristas in red and white costumes who were busily dispensing life-giving drinks to the lifeless-looking inhabitants of the chairs.

Opal sighed happily. "God, I love this place. Get me a Rudolph Special, will you? And Cole can have anything except the Jolly Fat Man donut surprise."

Cole giggled. "The surprise is I threw it up!"

Opal collapsed into a cushioned chair. "No, sweetie. It's three massive donuts cemented into a Santa the size of a toddler. You throwing it up after you scoffed it wasn't a surprise." She closed her eyes. *The surprise was you throwing it up on me while dive-bombing me when I was trying to put up the Christmas lights.*

"Gross, buddy." Jasper reached up to ruffle his nephew's hair. "You're right, your mom definitely deserves a coffee. Let's go get her one."

A few minutes later, Opal revived enough to grab the drink Jasper passed her. The Rudolph Special was the coffee cart's showstopper: a towering mug of whipped cream, caramel and raspberry syrup and chocolate flakes, all topped off with a bright red glace cherry.

Jasper had to assume there was coffee in there, somewhere under the sugar and cream, although there was no sign of it.

Cole buried his face in the snowman-shaped s'more cookie he had chosen. Jasper sat back in a chair next to his sister, a cup of *actual* coffee steaming in his hand. Well, mostly coffee. Maybe there was a bit of chocolate in it. And nutmeg. And a cinnamon stick poking out. And a big dollop of whipped cream. But hey— it was Christmas. What was he supposed to drink?

He heard Opal sigh before he felt the nudge of her telepathic voice against his mind. He squeezed his eyes shut for a moment, and let her in.

What's up, sis?

You know what's up, idiot. The rest of your life, for a start. Opal's mental voice was as grouchy as her real one, but even that couldn't hide the warmth and compassion behind her words. *I'm worried about you, bro. I know it's been hard for you, but... have you really given up hope?*

Jasper set down his coffee and stared into the glowing brazier. *I don't know what else to do, sis. If she was out there— wouldn't she have found me by now?*

Wouldn't I have found her? He winced at the pain that lanced through his mental voice. *Maybe I'm destined to be the fun, single uncle forever. I can live with that.*

Live with it as what, though? Opal's voice was gentle, but an undercurrent of concern ran through it.

Jasper went completely still.

Jasper, tell me you've thought about this. What are you going to choose?

What am I going to choose? Inside him, his dragon trembled. He reached for it, for the connection that had always been the core of his being, the place where man and dragon met— and for a moment, there was nothing.

Jasper let out his breath in a rush. Icy sweat beaded on his forehead. *That felt like— just for a moment, I thought—*

He gritted his teeth. Opal was right to be worried. This Christmas would be his twenty-fifth birthday. And like all Heartwell dragons, if he didn't find his mate before he turned twenty-five, he would have to make a terrible choice.

Only a mated Heartwell could hold on to both parts of their soul. If he didn't find his mate by Christmas, he would have to decide: to live the rest of his life as a dragon, or a man. And lose the other half of himself forever.

Jasper... Exasperation tinted Opal's mental voice. *You* have *decided, haven't you?*

Of course I have, Jasper lied. He jiggled his leg, unsettled, and then jumped up and prodded the brazier.

It was warm by the fire, but the evening was drawing in, and he shivered so hard he could almost feel his scales rattling. Or his skin goose-bumping. Either. Both. Did it really matter which, in the end? If he was going to be alone for the rest of his life, what did it matter what shape he was?

He turned away from Opal, not wanting her to see his face, and stared out across the square. Holiday shoppers drifted from shop to shop in small clusters, at least half of them trailing after scampering children. The air smelled like chocolate and coffee and spices, and was crisp with the promise of an icy night. The town lights were too bright here to see the stars, but he knew that out in the mountains, at the Heartwell lodge, they would be blazing down on the snowy peaks like fiery diamonds.

The Christmas lights shimmered and swam, and he blinked fiercely. He knew his destiny. He'd had all year for his suspicions to solidify into the grim truth that his fate was to be alone. Now all he had to do was convince Opal and the rest of his family that—

He blinked again. His gaze had drifted down from the sky as his eyes cleared, until he was staring out at the shopfront facades around the edge of the square. All the shops had gotten into the Christmas spirit, and the façades were a wonderland of fairy lights, fake snow, miniature trees and more Santas and reindeer than you could shake a candy cane at.

The shop his gaze had fallen on was even more festive than its neighbors. At ground level, everything was normal. Snowflake decals on the windows, a friendly snowman beckoning shoppers through the front door. But their rooftop display went above and beyond.

Balanced on the top of the roof, a massive Santa had dropped his sack and all the gifts were spilling out of it, cascading down the roof tiles as dozens of sparkly elves tried to catch them. The reindeer were getting in on the action— one was scarfing down a pile of cookies that had tipped out of a festive tin, and two others were fighting over a mega-sized cracker. Rudolph's front hooves were about to slip off the side. It was a scene of glorious, festive chaos... and Jasper wasn't seeing any of it.

Someone had propped a step-ladder against the eaves. A rotund Santa— slightly more real-looking than the giant on the roof— was holding it steady while a woman teetered on the top rung, reaching out towards the display.

Jasper froze. Inside him, his dragon uncurled like a whip, instantly alert. Jasper thought his heart would leap out of his chest. All he could hear was his pulse in his ears. He felt more alert, more *alive*, than he had in months.

"It's her," he said, the words out before his brain had finished forming them. *Her.* His destiny. His mate.

She was facing away from the square, but as he watched, she turned her head to call something down to the man in the Santa outfit who was holding the ladder in place. Just that glimpse of her face hit Jasper like a blow to the heart.

The woman had a small, upturned nose and large, expressive eyes. Her cheeks were pink with exertion or the cold or both, and her lips were wide and red. Light brown hair escaped from under her elf-hat to frame her face and spill down over her shoulders.

She was dressed like one of Santa's elves, in an apple-green tunic that hugged her curves and candy-stripe stockings. Jasper couldn't help imagining how her legs would look as she climbed back down the ladder. Her shiny red shoes looked secure on the rungs, but maybe she would need a steadying hand as she made it back down to the ground— *his* hand, caressing the thick curves of her calves, sliding up the backs of her thighs— all to help balance her, of course… no ulterior motives…

"Jasper?"

He heard Opal climb out of the low armchair, but he didn't turn around. He couldn't. He was caught, pinned in place by wonder.

"Jasper, what are you— oh." Tentative joy bubbled into Opal's voice. "Is she— really? *Now?*" She clutched at his arm. "What are you going to do?"

"Fall in love with her."

"That's only half the equation, Jas. She has to fall for you, too. And it's only five days until your birthday!"

"Five days during the most wonderful time of the year," Jasper reminded her. Certainty blazed inside him like a bonfire, burning away all the fear and resignation that had built up over the last months. "This is it, Opal, I know it. It's all going to work out. After all, I'm a Christmas dragon. And who doesn't like Christmas?"

2

ABIGAIL

Abigail swore under her breath as the ladder teetered. "I *hate* Christmas," she muttered.

She glared at the rooftop display. It was all set up to look like it was about to come crashing down on the road below— well, right now she wished it would come tumbling down on *her*.

"All right up there, Abby-babby?"

Abigail forced a smile over gritted teeth. "I'm fine, Mr. Bell! Just so long as you keep the ladder steady!" She winced at the sing-song sound of her own voice in full retail-assistant mode. "Almost got it…"

She glanced down at her boss to reassure herself that he was still holding the ladder in place on the slippery paving stones, and turned back to her task. Near the bottom of the ridiculous display, almost close enough for her to reach, was a beribboned gift box with an adorable kitten poking its head out.

It was fake, of course. Same as everything else about this time of year. But that hadn't stopped her boss' heart from melting when some apple-cheeked little asshole started crying that someone had to *save* the poor kitten, it was so *scared* and *cold* and *look,* it has *snow* on it!

Well, either his heart had melted at the kid, or other parts of his anatomy had reacted to the kid's bombshell mother.

And so, in the spirit of the season, Mr. Bell had dispatched Abigail to "save" the poor "kitten".

Standing on tip-toe on the top rung of the ladder, Abigail could almost reach the pathetic stuffed animal. If she leaned— *ugh*— her breasts brushed up against the cold, wet tiles, but she could just wrap one finger around the toy's outstretched little paw.

"Come on, you little— aha!"

Abigail slithered back until her feet were flat on the ladder again, the kitten toy safely in her grasp. The wet, freezing cold kitten toy. She gave it a half-hearted shake and a flurry of icy droplets merrily soaked into her chest.

Merry Christmas, Abigail, she groaned silently. Out loud, she called, "Got it! I'm coming down, boss!"

Mr. Bell didn't reply. Trying to ignore the cold water dripping onto her from the kitten toy, she peered down at the street. Mr. Bell was still there, and so was the little kid who'd been so concerned about kitty's welfare… and so was the kid's mom. Who had a waterfall of gold-blonde hair, and a laugh like jingle bells, and a figure that filled out her puffy winter coat in a way that Abigail was sure should be illegal. Not that Abigail was jealous, or anything.

Mr Bell was staring at her transfixed, leaning absent-mindedly against the ladder.

Oh, come on. Seriously?

"Uh, Mr. Bell?" He didn't look up— but he did lean more of his weight on the ladder. "Mr. Bell!"

Abigail held on tight to the ladder and clambered down as fast as she could, but it wasn't fast enough. Everything seemed to go into slow motion.

Mr. Bell puffed out his chest at the blonde woman. The ladder's feet skidded sideways on the slick pavement. Abigail was suddenly, sickeningly, airborne.

But not, she knew, for long.

She fell backwards, the sky swooping overhead. Cold wind whipped at her legs. The kitten toy stared glumly at her from her right hand. She noted absently that one of its eyes had fallen out.

Somewhere below her and to her left, the ladder crashed down on the ground. She could only be a split-second from impact herself. Abigail squeezed her eyes shut. Some stupid, ridiculous part of her wanted to cover the kitten's remaining eye, as well. As though that would help.

"Oof!"

Abigail cracked one eye open. Christmas lights spun above her, looping down from the shop's eaves.

She wasn't dead. She opened her other eye cautiously. The lights kept spinning, but they slowed down. Stopped.

What just happened?

Maybe she'd landed on her boss? But she could feel strong arms holding her, and the face staring down into hers wasn't the squashed ghost of Henry Bell. It was a man she'd never seen before. A *gorgeous* man.

He had his arms around her. He was *holding* her. Carrying her like she weighed as little as the poor wet kitten toy, and hadn't just hurtled out of the sky like a mad, red-and-green meteor.

"Hi," the man said, and Abigail's heart turned over. This guy wasn't Mr. Bell. He wasn't squashed. What he was, was the most breath-stoppingly handsome man she'd ever laid eyes on.

He had dark hair that swooped over his forehead, and eyes that looked a rich, warm brown— but she must have been in shock, because they looked different colors as well, red and gold spinning in their depths like sparks flying out of a roaring fire.

His cheeks were flushed with exertion, his cheeks were dusted with a day's dark stubble and his lips were red and looked temptingly soft.

Temptingly soft— and only a few inches away from her own. Abigail was suddenly intensely, painfully aware of the man's arms around her. He was holding her to his chest, which meant she could *feel* his chest through the thin fabric of her work costume, and oh God, it was a really nice chest. Just like his face was a really nice face, and his arms felt like really nice arms, and—

"Hi," she said at last, her cheeks blazing.

"Are you all right?" His voice was warm and mellow, like molten chocolate drizzled over butterscotch ice cream. Abigail licked her lips.

"I—" Cold water dripped down her arm, and she looked down to see the kitten toy's single eye staring woefully at her. "I got the thing!"

"You got the— ?"

Abigail wriggled upright and the man let her go, setting her safely on her feet. Adrenaline, or maybe just the joy of not being splatted on the ground, filled Abigail's body until her skin felt like it was about to start fizzing. She turned to Mr. Bell, the kid, and the kid's mom, all of whom were staring at her wide-eyed.

"Here," she said, grinning at the kid and holding out the toy. "I brought kitty down, just like you wanted. Do you want to take her with you? I could dry her off out back, if you like—"

The kid grabbed at the toy and then recoiled. "Ewww! It's all *gross*! Mom, I don't want it, it's *yucky!*"

"Well, yeah, it's been up on the roof for about a month now..." Abigail began, and then bit her tongue as Mr. Bell shot her a warning glare. He turned back to the customers, a buttery smile melting across his face.

"Now, now, I'm sure we can get this all sorted out—"

"It's *yucky!* I want a *nice* kitty!"

"Yes, sweetie, let's go and get you a nice kitty somewhere else." A familiar expression passed over the blonde woman's face: part exhaustion, part irritation at the incompetency of retail workers, part fear that her daughter was about to make a scene. She tugged at her daughter's mittened hand. "Maybe at that shop back across the road?"

Mr. Bell's greasy smile melted off completely as the blonde woman sashayed away. Abigail wasn't sure exactly how she managed to sashay in a winter coat and snow boots, but she did it somehow.

Abigail sighed. "So much for the poor, lonely kitten— hey!"

She jumped back as Mr. Bell shook his finger under her nose.

"What do you think you're doing? First you almost flatten this poor gentleman, and now you're just going to stand there like a stunned fish? Go inside and get changed! I don't want you losing me any *more* sales!" His eyes narrowed to angry, sweaty slits under his Santa hat and stick-on eyebrows.

Abigail opened her mouth to ask whether he'd really been intending to *charge* the woman and her daughter for the sodden soft toy, and then closed it again. What was the point? It was Christmas; he'd only find something else to complain about.

"Sorry, boss," she muttered, and Mr. Bell stomped back into the shop, gesturing angrily for Abigail to follow him..

All her adrenaline-fueled exhilaration drained away. Abigail's shoulders slumped. She wasn't sure what she'd expected; praise for going above and beyond? An apology for almost making her fall to her death? Hell, had Mr. Bell even *noticed* the danger she had been in— or just the possible risk to his sales margin?

Didn't I learn this lesson years ago? Never put yourself out there. Not for anyone, and definitely not at Christmas.

She looked down at the soaking-wet cat toy in her hand and grimaced. Now she had to deal with this, as well. And—

"Is he meant to be Santa, or the Grinch?" said a warm, deep voice behind her. Abigail's heart jumped into her throat.

He was still there. Her rescuer.

She turned around, trying to look casual, and realized too late that she was still holding the plush toy out in front of her. The wet bundle of faux fur slapped into her rescuer's jacket.

"Oh, God, I'm so sorry," she blurted out, snatching her hand back. "I didn't mean to— um, I didn't..." The man's eyes creased with amusement, and she forced herself to relax. She stuck out her hand— the one without the toy in it. "Thanks, uh, for saving me from becoming a festive splat on the ground."

He pulled off his glove before shaking her hand. His fingers closed around hers gently, and her shoulders tingled with the memory of his arm wrapped around them.

His other arm— and hand— had been wrapped around her legs. As soon as she remembered that, her thighs started tingling, too. She bit her lip, forcing herself not to look away from his strangely multicolored eyes.

Don't blush, she ordered herself. Don't blush. Wow, his eyes really are beautiful...

"I'm Jasper," the man said.

Like his eyes, Abigail thought, feeling dizzy.

"Are you all right?" Jasper stepped closer, concern darkening his eyes. "That was some fall. I'm—" He swallowed. "I'm glad I was passing by."

Me too. Abigail's head buzzed, and the words stuck in her throat. What was wrong with her? Just talk to him like a normal person. Not like he's the most handsome man who's ever… touched you. Oh, God.

Her skin tingled as she remembered how it had felt to have his arms around her. He'd appeared out of nowhere, and saved her life. Like a miracle.

Really? A Christmas miracle? You're really going to go there?

This wasn't a miracle. It was some guy who'd been in the right place at the right time, and was now probably desperate to get on with whatever he'd been doing before she fell out of the sky and onto him.

Abigail felt like someone had just dumped ice-water down her back.

He'd just been going about his business, she'd almost splatted him, and now she was practically drooling at him in the middle of the street. She remembered Mr. Bell's glazed eyes staring at the blonde woman who'd been after a present for her daughter, and felt sick.

"I'm fine," she said quickly. She knew she should go inside and leave the poor guy alone, but her feet felt glued in place.

The guy— Jasper— was still looking at her, one eyebrow raised. "So, what were you doing up that ladder, anyway?"

Abigail blinked. He could just leave, but he hadn't.

Did he… actually want to stop and talk with her?

Abigail bit her lip. Technically, she was still on duty. Her shift didn't end for another few hours. But, *also* technically, Jasper was a potential customer. Talking to him was her job.

And maybe a short chat would give her time for her heart to stop racing, and her feet to un-glue from the sidewalk.

She glanced up at the man. He was staring at her mouth, his cheeks slightly flushed.

"I was getting this thing down." Abigail held up the soft toy, and Jasper's eyes flicked to it—guilty-fast. Her heart flipped, but she managed to keep her voice even. "Kid went on and *on* about it, but the moment it's out of the gift box, she didn't want it any more. Which is Christmas in a nutshell, isn't it?"

"Are Christmas kittens a thing now?" Jasper frowned. "I'm going to have to rethink my whole gifting plan for my nephew..." His eyes sparkled, and Abigail started to feel herself unwind. Maybe

Abigail snorted. "Nope. Kitty here is a leftover from Halloween." She held it up so he could see the tiny pumpkin shapes the toy had instead of toes. "See? And it's already falling apart. Poor kitty. We should have dumped you straight in the garbage with all the other leftovers."

"That's a bit harsh." Jasper leaned closer, and Abigail's face started to feel hot. He poked at the soft toy, carefully inspecting it. "It's not in that bad condition— oh. What happened to its other eye? Um, whoops."

He raised his hands and backed away as the leg he'd been playfully shaking came loose. Abigail laughed and picked it up.

"See? It's a hopeless case. Straight in the bin." She glanced back up at the roof. Her fall hadn't disturbed any of the rest of the display. Still the same leering elves and giant, drunk-looking Santa. "Along with the rest of that rubbish as soon as Christmas is over."

"Aw, where's your Christmas spirit?" he said, laughing.

Abigail raised her eyebrows at him. "I think Mr. Bell sold it earlier today. Fifty percent off. Which is a great deal, because I've never gotten much use out of it."

She'd meant it as a joke, but Jasper's face fell. Guilt shot through her. The guy had just saved her life— and, oh God, she was going to remember the sensation of his arms around her for as long as she lived— and now she'd gone and messed that up, too.

Why was she always like this? She hated Christmas, sure, but that didn't mean she had to ruin it for everyone else.

Especially since she was still technically at work.

She forced a smile onto her face. "Hey, I'm kidding. It's just, you know—"

"You don't like Christmas?" Jasper sounded confused. She stared at him.

"I'm not its biggest fan, no." *Drop it, please,* she added silently.

"But—" He spread his arms, gesturing to the over-decorated town square. The giant fake tree, the ridiculous strings of fire-hazard Christmas lights. All the harried shoppers, desperate for the latest bargain.

Abigail didn't know what made her open her mouth. Maybe it was the shock of falling off the roof. *Or maybe you're just a terrible person.*

"But what? You think anyone out there is really having fun?" A muscle in her jaw twitched and she wrapped her arms tightly around herself. "It's all *fake.* Look at them all, stressing out over buying presents that will be forgotten a day later. Acting like all these carols don't make you want to claw your ears off. Putting on a happy face and holding it together so the kiddies can experience the *magic of Christmas.*"

She bit her lips shut before she could say anything else. Bitterness surged through her— but it felt good, too, to say it out loud. Let out all the frustration that had been building inside of her for so long.

Abigail turned back to Jasper, and her stomach fell. He looked like someone had just slapped him. *And that someone is you, genius.*

She opened her mouth, ready to apologize, when Mr. Bell's voice cut through the air.

"Abby-babby!" Abigail winced. Mr. Bell pushed through the door, a smile on his face for Jasper— who, after all, might turn out to be a customer— and a scowl for Abigail. "I thought I told you to go out back. Or wasn't that stunt with the ladder enough for you? You wanna put on another show?"

"What?" Abigail's forehead creased— and then she followed Mr. Bell's gaze down to the front of her costume. "Oh."

Her little skid down the rooftop might not have disturbed the display, but it had left a huge wet patch all down her front. The thin polyester elf costume was clinging to her boobs. The only reason she hadn't felt it was because it must not have soaked through her shapewear yet... but it was only a matter of time. And in the meantime, she was giving the whole square a show.

"Oh, *shit*," she muttered, wiping futilely at her tunic.

Mr. Bell almost exploded. "Inside. *Now!*"

Abigail put her head down, cheeks blazing with shame, and made for the door.

"Wait!"

Arms cradling her wet-stained chest, Abigail spun back to Jasper.

What now? she wanted to scream. What can possibly make this day worse, than being screamed at by children, almost falling to my death, and being yelled at by my boss in front of the hottest guy I've ever met?

"What time does your shift end?"

Abigail gaped. Of all the questions she'd expected, this hadn't even made the top hundred. Was he serious? Was this hot guy— who's just *saved her life*— asking her out? At Christmas?

That was impossible. Worse than impossible. At Christmas? She couldn't risk it.

"I can't—" she began, and then Mr. Bell shouted again. She put her head down and ran inside, desperately trying to convince herself she was doing the right thing.

The rest of her shift was busy, but it was the mindless sort of busy that left her brain a lot of time to think up better answers to Jasper's question. Answers like *Ten o'clock,* or the more accurate *Ten o'clock unless Mr. Bell decides we need to stay open late again,* or the crazy but heartfelt *Right now! Let's go! Screw you, Mr. Bell, I quit!*

But of course she wasn't going to quit. If she was, she would have handed in her notice back in October, when they started putting up Christmas decorations, and found another job to fill up the days before Christmas.

And it was too late to think of other things she could have said now, anyway. Jasper had his answer: Abigail George was a crazy lady. Stay away. *Especially during the holiday season.*

She shook her head.

"You all right, hon?" A candy-cane prodded Abigail in the nose. She looked up into her workmate Carol's inquiring gaze.

Abigail hoisted a smile onto her face. "I'm fine," she said, trying to sound as upbeat as Carol always did. "Long day."

"Well, they're only going to get longer!" Carol chirped. "I can't believe you took on *all* the late shifts. But I guess it's not like you have family waiting at home for you."

"You know, Carol, that is *so* true." Abigail's smile was starting to freeze.

"This is my last late shift before Christmas, thank God." Carol hooked another candy cane over the store's Christmas tree. It had started the day fully stocked, but had been stripped bare to waist-height by hordes of hungry children. And above-waist-height by all the adults who didn't want to miss out on free candy. "Really, Abigail, thank you so much for volunteering. I don't know what I'd do if I had to work extra... Are you saving up to buy something for someone special?"

"Mm-hmm," Abigail murmured non-commitally.

There was no way she was going to tell bubbly, friendly Carol the truth. The extra shifts weren't about saving up *for* anything. More like saving herself *from* something— and that something, ironically enough, was Christmas.

Carol made a show of looking at her watch. "Well, he should be here soon, anyway."

"What? Who?"

"Your *someone special,* silly!" Carol thwapped her with a candy cane. "I saw Mr. Bell hurry you away before you could finish talking with him, so I nipped out and let him know when your shift ended."

"You mean Jasper?" Abigail's skin tingled.

"Oh, is that his name? He is *gorgeous,* isn't he? Honestly, if I didn't have my Matt at home, I would have half a mind to steal him off you. Mind you, my children would probably kick up a fuss. And the grandchildren, bless them." Carol placed her final candy cane on the tree and sighed happily. "There, that's done. Anything else on the checklist?"

"Huh? Oh, um..." Abigail grabbed the clipboard and stared at it. She was so off-kilter, she didn't even roll her eyes at the words along the top of the page: *Check it twice!* Did everything need to be a reference to a carol or Christmas story? "We cashed up already, so it's just setting the timer on the lights, and locking up."

She hardly heard herself. Her mind felt like it was full of cotton wool. *Jasper? Here? End of my shift? But that's now!*

She looked down at herself. Carol, who was a legitimate sweetheart, had lent her a Christmas sweater to cover the wet stain on her work outfit. It covered the stain all right, but it also looked like it had been knitted out of tinsel. She looked like something Rudolph had thrown up.

And she didn't have a change of clothes.

She'd been planning to go straight home, strip off, and collapse into a dead sleep until half an hour before the start of her next shift. Her usual Christmas season routine. Her system.

Her system worked. But it had never, ever had to make space for anyone else in it before. Let alone a handsome man like Jasper, whose chest she could still almost feel pressing against her own. Whose arms...

Someone knocked on the front window. Abigail turned around, ready to tell them to come back in the morning, and stopped with her mouth open. Jasper was standing outside, two steaming takeaway cups in his hands and an enchanting smile on his face.

"Oh, no," Abigail muttered under her breath.

Carol tapped her on the arm. "You go, hon. I'll finish up here. It's the least I could do, with you taking all those extra shifts."

"I, uh." Abigail's brain scrambled for words. "I'll just be one minute!"

She waved to Jasper, and darted out the back. Her bag was hanging on its hook in the staff corner like always, but that wasn't what she was looking for. Abigail fought her way past a pile of flattened cardboard boxes and tangled webs of tinsel. She was sure it was here somewhere—

"Aha!" She cried out in triumph and held the dress aloft. It wasn't haute couture, and she wouldn't look half as good in it as the blonde woman had looked in her cute little winter outfit… but at least it wasn't an elf costume.

3

JASPER

Jasper blinked as Abigail stepped out onto the sidewalk. She looked beautiful, of course. Her hair peeked out from under a navy-blue beanie, and her winter coat was sensible, long and quilted in a matching navy. But he hadn't been expecting what he could see under it.

"What happened to the tinsel sweater?" he asked, trying not to sound disappointed. He'd glimpsed it through the window, a gloriously silly confection of gold and red and green sparkles. And, of course, the candy-stripe stockings underneath her tunic…

"That monstrosity?" Abigail bit her lip guiltily and looked back into the shop. Her co-worker gave her the thumbs-up. "Uh, Carol let me borrow it for the rest of my shift. It's not mine."

Jasper frowned. "Don't tell me you're still wearing the elf dress, then. You'll freeze out here."

"Oh, it's mostly dried out by now. But don't worry, I'm not going to wear that ridiculous thing on a d—" Abigail broke off, her cheeks blazing.

Inside him, Jasper's dragon flexed its wings smugly. "Uh, um. Anyway. I found this out back."

She unzipped her coat and held it open. Jasper's eyes widened. *Wow.*

"Let me guess," he said, unable to tear his eyes away. "Something else leftover from Halloween?"

Abigail laughed out loud. The sound sent fireworks off in his brain. "Very Morticia Addams, right? And a bit more suitable for a… night out than some dinky elf costume." The corner of her mouth twitched down, too quickly and too small a movement for it to be intentional.

"Oh, I don't know. I liked the costume. Especially the hat." Not that he didn't like the figure-hugging, floor-length black dress she had on now. *Wow.*

"Well, I'm sorry to break it to you. The hat is for shop hours only."

"Then I guess I'll have to come back and see you tomorrow."

She shrugged, but a smile fought its way onto her lips. "It's your funeral."

A tremor struck Jasper. He forced a laugh, hoping she hadn't noticed. Because she was right. If she didn't accept him before his birthday, it would be the end of him. Human, or dragon. One way or the other, part of him would cease to exist.

"Well, so much for my tomorrow plans," he said breezily. "As for tonight…" He let the sentence fade away. Abigail looked up at him, her eyes bright but wary. "As for tonight, and our d— night out…"

"Oh, stop it," she complained, shoving her hands into her pockets and ducking her head.

"As for our *date*, because I *am* taking you on a date— I think it's the least you owe me for saving your life, by the way— I thought I'd start by buying you a drink. Here." He handed her one of the takeaway cups.

She took it, and happiness unfurled inside him. His first gift to her, and she'd accepted it.

"What is this?"

"I'll be honest," Jasper said, peeking under the lid of his own cup, "I'm not entirely sure. I *asked* for standard egg nog, but my nephew started whispering to the barista while I was paying, and now I'm noticing the distinct smell of…" He sniffed.

"Mint?" Abigail took a sip. "And…"

"Orange." Jasper looked at her. "I am so, so sorry."

She took another gulp. "No, it's, um. Ooh." She grimaced, and then shrugged. "Well, it's definitely not Christmassy."

His heart twisted. He should have checked before he brought them over. She was going to reject it, and it was his fault.

Abigail met his eyes. "You know what? I've been on my feet all day, except for a brief period of flying through the air, and this might be— *interesting*— but, the hell with it." She upended the cup and drained the rest of the drink, swallowing with another grimace. "Yum. How old is your nephew, by the way?"

"Cole. He's four."

She nodded, staring into the bottom of her cup. "Makes sense. Also, there's half a candy cane in the bottom of this, so that explains the mint." She nodded at his cup. "Come on— bottoms up!"

Jasper swigged back the mint-orange nog, every atom of his body singing. She'd accepted it. It was terrible, and he made a mental note not to let Cole near the kitchen unsupervised while Christmas prep was happening, but—

"Bleugh," he said, wiping his mouth. "I would say it grows on you, but…"

"It really doesn't?" She laughed. "Hey, you missed a bit."

Jasper held still as she reached up and brushed her thumb against the corner of his mouth. Her touch was electric.

She paused, eyes wide, as though her hand had moved ahead of her brain, and her mind was only just realizing what she'd done. Jasper took advantage of her hesitation. He turned his head, and kissed the smear of orange-mint-nog off her thumb.

"Mmm," he murmured. "You know, maybe it isn't so bad. Could be a new Christmas tradition."

Abigail's eyes shuttered. "Pff," she snorted. "Sweet, fake and disgusting? Sure, sounds like Christmas to me." She pulled her hand away and shoved it deep into her pocket.

Jasper's heart sank. "That's right. You're not a huge fan of Christmas, huh?"

"Not so much." Abigail's voice was crisp.

"There's nothing about it that you like? Not even Christmas trees?" She shook her head. "Stockings? Candy canes? Snow? Egg nog?"

Abigail laughed. "I think I prefer your nephew's version." She hesitated, and then burst out: "I mean, it's all fake, isn't it? At least that nog was *genuinely* terrible."

Jasper sagged. His mate didn't like Christmas? But he was the Christmas dragon. And if she hated everything about the holiday season, how was he meant to win her over before his deadline?

His connection with his dragon trembled. He rubbed his hands together, trying to hide the worry inside him.

"So much for my big date plans," he joked.

"Plans?" Abigail blinked, and looked down at her empty takeaway cup. A line formed between her eyebrows. "I thought— I mean, you brought me this…"

And you thought that was it? Jasper frowned. Inside him, his dragon hissed smoke. That was *unacceptable*.

His mate deserved more than a terrible drink. She deserved to *expect* more from a date than a terrible drink.

Not that she's going to be dating anyone except me.

Certainty settled around Jasper like a warm, fuzzy Christmas sweater. He was going to woo his mate. He had five days to make her the happiest woman in the world, and if she didn't think this was the most wonderful time of the year… then he would have to win her over without relying on his Christmas charms. It couldn't be that hard— right?

"Come on," he said, and slipped his hand under her elbow. "I'm going to take you to dinner."

Dinner. Easy, right? *Wrong.* Everywhere Jasper looked, Christmas stared back at him. Carols filtered out through the streets. Restaurants advertised special, holiday-themed menus. And all the decorations. Tinsel. Fairy lights. Snowflakes, model sleighs, red-cheeked Santas and red-nosed Rudolphs…

And Abigail's hand in his.

Oh, he'd started off holding her arm. Very gentlemanly and proper. But as they walked, he had slid his hand lower— lower— and, after all, she wasn't wearing gloves, so it was only right that he helped her keep her hand warm, on a cold night like this…

The moment his fingers had brushed up against hers, Abigail had leaned against him. Her face had lit up. And now they were walking together, so close they were almost tripping over each other's feet, with her hand in his, tucked snugly into his coat pocket.

They had been walking for almost an hour, up and down streets festooned with strings of lights and smelling of cinnamon and nutmeg. The air was crisp; Jasper was sure that by midnight, the paper snowflakes hanging in the street-front windows would be joined by real ice crystals growing at the corners of the glass. Any other night, he would have reveled in the Christmassy atmosphere. Tonight, though, he was looking for *not* Christmas.

And he thought he had just found it.

"There!"

"Where?"

Jasper pointed. They were at the edge of the residential part of town, where restaurants and shops made way for houses and low apartment buildings. The decorations were less intense, but more heart-warming— strings of streamers and cut-out Christmas scenes, handmade with love.

Except for one house.

Jasper pointed it out to Abigail. On the far corner of the next four-way intersection was a two-floor apartment building. The ground floor was sparkling with lights, but the top level was completely bare. No lights, no tinsel, no Santa decals, not the slightest hint of Christmas. Just a dark, plain apartment.

"Voila!" Jasper swooped his pointing-finger through the air, drawing Abigail's attention to the small restaurant opposite the Christmas-free zone. "See that table in the front window? The cunning orientation of the street signs, and that parked van? If we sit *there*, we won't be able to see anything Christmassy. Just that one undecorated house, and the stars in the night sky." He looked up. "Well, maybe not the stars, the streetlights are a bit bright for that. But we can imagine."

Abigail gave him a strange look, one eyebrow quirked up. "Really? Here?"

Jasper huffed out his breath theatrically. "We *could* go back to that place on the last block— you remember, the one with the troupe of singing Santas…"

Abigail shuddered. "No, it's okay, it's just this is…" She grinned impishly, squeezing his fingers. "This is fine, actually."

Luckily, the restaurant was still open, even though it was past eleven. Jasper inhaled deeply as he held the door open for his mate. His stomach growled.

He had eaten dinner with Opal and Cole earlier, but that had been hours ago. "This place smells delicious. What is it?"

"They do— I mean, it looks like they do Dutch food." Abigail smiled, tucking in her lips like she was hiding a secret. "You know, I already had a sandwich on my dinner break. If you're happy to just make this a dessert date…"

"Yes. A hundred times yes." His stomach growled again, louder this time. Abigail giggled. "Sooner rather than later. I think my stomach is ready to stage a rebellion after that nog."

Abigail tugged on his hand, leading him to the window table. "Wow, you're right," she said brightly as they sat down. "No decorations in sight. Good choice."

Jasper glanced around the inside of the restaurant. "So long as you keep looking outside," he said, noting the rows of festive wreaths on the walls.

"Got it." Abigail smiled at him and his heart lit up. This was working. Everything was going to be fine. He had found his mate— and he would keep both parts of his soul. Both parts of *him*. He wouldn't need to sacrifice anything. "So, what'll you have?"

Jasper tore his eyes away from her long enough to peer at the menu. "Everything," he decided.

"These are delicious." Jasper speared another poffertje, the bite-sized, buttery, puffy pancakes sprinkled with icing sugar. He held up his fork. "Have you tried them?"

Abigail giggled through a mouthful of apple tart. She covered her mouth with her hand and swallowed before she replied. "Oh, only about twenty. So far. This evening."

Jasper waved his pancake-laden fork entreatingly and she rolled her eyes.

"Oh, well, if you insist…"

She lowered her hand. Cheeks pink, she opened her mouth.

Her lips were red and soft. She licked them, and they glistened temptingly. Jasper's heart ached. *Five days*.

He carefully lifted the fork to her lips, and held back a groan as she pulled the tiny pancake off it with her teeth. She chewed it slowly, eyes closed, and then swallowed and licked her lips again. *Oh, God.*

"You know," she said consideringly, looking up at him from under lowered lashes, "I think that was the best of the lot." She paused. "Was it the last one?"

"Afraid so." Jasper scanned the table. They'd ordered everything on the menu, and lingered over every bite, but now there was nothing left. Not even a crumb.

He raised his eyes to the beautiful woman sitting opposite him. She had hung up her coat behind the door, and her curves were on full display in the figure-hugging black Halloween dress. The neckline plunged deeper than he would have imagined appropriate for a work outfit, and— *Oh, God*— a few flecks of icing sugar had fallen onto Abigail's cleavage, like a light dusting of snow. He clenched his hands on the edge of the table, resisting the urge to lean over and lick the sugar off.

He didn't want the night to end. Or if it had to, he wanted it to end with Abigail in his arms.

Jasper bit back a heartfelt groan. He couldn't take her home. His family lodge was hours away, up a long mountain road and… he didn't have a car. *Damn it.*

"I guess this is it." Abigail's voice was halting, as though she didn't want their date to end, either. She glanced up at him, and her cheeks went pink.

Jasper leaned forward. Maybe he couldn't take her to bed tonight, but he could at least make his intentions clear. She'd been so surprised when he asked her out, and even more so when he turned up at the end of her shift. As though she hadn't believed he would be there.

He needed her to know that he would be there for her, every night for the rest of his life.

Jasper slid one hand across the table towards Abigail. She glanced at it, startled, and then slowly reached out with her own hand. Her fingers closed over his tentatively and she looked up at him, a question in her eyes.

She opened her mouth, and hesitated. Jasper waited as she swallowed hard, her fingers tightening over his.

"I feel like I'm waiting for the other shoe to drop," she said in an undertone, a line forming between her eyebrows. "All this— the drink, dinner, an actual *date*… This never happens to me." She bit her lip and looked away, frowning at the table.

"It's happening now," Jasper said softly.

"You *say* that," Abigail muttered, "but I'm still having trouble believing it." She looked up at him. "This could all be some sort of retail-induced fever dream. Maybe I'm still behind the counter back at the shop, serving midnight customers."

"Or maybe," Jasper began, running his finger through the icing sugar on the poffertje plate, "Maybe you're right here."

He lifted his finger to her lips. Her eyes widened with shock— and then went dark, her pupils wide with desire. She opened her mouth. Her lips glistened, and she leaned forward, just enough to touch the tip of her tongue to Jasper's finger.

He went hard so fast it hurt.

Abigail sat back fast, her cheeks burning. "I…" She looked up at him and licked her lips. A sudden wild look flashed through her eyes, and then was replaced by burning determination. "Are you doing anything… else… tonight?"

Jasper leaned further forward. "You tell me."

"Oh. *Oh.*" Abigail's lips parted. She looked dazed—and then her eyes focused on his. He saw the moment she made up her mind. "Would you like to, um. Head across the road to my place?"

Her eyes widened, as though she couldn't believe what she had just said. Jasper felt her tense, like a deer about to bolt. He caught her hand between both of his, raising it to kiss her fingertips— and then her words sank in.

"Wait… across the road?" Jasper stared at her like an idiot.

The corners of Abigail's mouth quirked up, and she nodded out to the dark, undecorated apartment across the street.

"That's…" Jasper groaned and hung his head. "Oh, God. I walked you all around town, and we ended up at your local?"

At the back of the restaurant, behind the counter, the waiter sniggered. Abigail glared at him. "Mind your own business, Gustaaf!"

"And bring us the check, please!" Jasper added.

Abigail caught his eye. Her lips parted, and for just a moment, she looked uncertain. Jasper pulled her hand to his lips. The uncertainty in her eyes faded, replaced by sparkling excitement.

Jasper whipped the check away when it arrived, ignoring Abigail's protests. Dinner was *absolutely* on him. His dragon wouldn't have it any other way.

Gustaaf waved at them as they left. "Hey, Abigail! Merry—" He laughed as Abigail shot him a dirty look. "Have a good night," he finished, and cackled.

Abigail rolled her eyes as they stepped back onto the street. "Oh, he is never going to shut up about this. I've just given him gossip for weeks." She paused. "*And* his Nan. Oh, God."

"Having second thoughts?" The idea of Abigail taking him home on their first night appealed, he had to admit— God, that was putting it lightly— but he didn't want to pressure her into anything.

Abigail grabbed his hand. "Hell, no." She laughed, ducking her head. "Hey, the universe literally threw me into your arms… who am I to argue with that?"

4
ABIGAIL

Abigail's heart beat like a drum in her chest. *What the hell am I doing?*

Never tell a guy you liked him. That was the rule, wasn't it? The rule that had served Abigail very well so far… in her life as a single lady, who lived by herself, opposite an all-night pancake parlor.

And never ask for anything at Christmas. Never even hint that there's anything you want. You'll only be disappointed.

But she'd never liked someone the way she liked Jasper before. Even her stupid high-school crushes hadn't been as sudden and overwhelming as what she felt for him.

And none of them had liked her back. Whereas Jasper… oh, God. She couldn't be imagining it, could she? The way he looked at her?

Her chest thudded as she waited for Jasper to respond. Even after all the time they'd spent together this evening, she didn't really believe he could be interested in her. Or maybe she just couldn't *let* herself believe it.

Time seemed to stretch out, even though she knew it couldn't have been more than a few seconds.

"Well then," Jasper said, his voice like molten chocolate. "You'd better take me home."

Red and gold flared in the depths of his eyes. Abigail swayed forward. She tried to tell herself it was because she wanted to look at his eyes more carefully, see how this trick of the light and colors really worked— but she knew that wasn't the truth. She moved towards him because she wanted his touch, wanted the feeling of her hand enclosed in his but all over her body. She wanted her skin to thrill at his touch, wanted the edgy excitement inside her to bloom into hot need and—

She took a quick step forward. Her hands made fists in the front of his winter coat, pulling him closer, pulling him down to her so his face was level with hers. A soft moan escaped her lips and then she was kissing him, his lips soft against hers but not pliant— he was kissing her back, his tongue flicking out against her lower lip, his arms folding around her and holding her tight.

The world around them disappeared. The cold night, the stupid, fake decorations, all faded away. There was nothing but the hot tenderness of Jasper's mouth on hers, the taste of icing sugar on his lips, the strength of his arms around her... and the promise of his body under far too many layers of clothing.

Stupid Christmas. Stupid winter. Why couldn't they have met in the summer? She bet Jasper looked incredible in a bathing suit. Or less.

Her fingers tightened on his coat. "Go?" she murmured into his lips.

He didn't say anything; his grin against her lips was answer enough.

It shouldn't be this hard to unlock a door when I'm sober, Abigail thought as she wrestled with her key. At least the door clicked open. Just in time. Jasper's fingers were snaking around her jaw, pulling her in for another kiss. She just managed to trip backwards into her apartment and kick the door shut behind them before he flicked his tongue against her lips and every sensible thought disappeared from her mind.

She had a coat rack. She ignored it. Her winter jacket hit the floor, and the sensation of Jasper's hands whispering against her sides was so intense she almost forgot to help him with his coat, too. Like a good hostess.

Her fingers fumbled at his buttons. One. Two. Too many. At last the heavy coat fell away and revealed… a Christmas sweater.

With… dancing Christmas trees on it?

Abigail groaned. There was only one thing to do with this. *Off.*

The sweater disappeared into a far corner of her apartment, knocking something over. *Too bad. So long as it's gone…*

Abigail ran her hands down Jasper's chest, feeling his pecs through the thin fabric of his shirt. A moan escaped his mouth as her fingers ghosted over his abs. And lower. Suddenly his hands were hard on her waist, pulling her to him.

"Bedroom?" he gasped into his ear, and heat bloomed inside her.

She grabbed his belt buckle and tugged. "This way."

It wasn't far. Her apartment was only a dozen paces end-to-end. She could usually stumble from the front door to her bedroom in seven steps. Tonight, it took her zero steps, because Jasper carried her.

He set her down at her bedroom door and kissed her again. Desire flooded her veins. Her skin was on fire, and the only thing that would quench it was his touch. Skin to skin.

She pushed him back until the backs of his legs bumped against her bed. Still kissing him, she let her hands wander: over his chest, his sides, venturing under the hem of his t-shirt. Heat blossomed between her legs as she felt bare skin under her fingers.

Jasper moaned as she ran her fingertips along his skin, tracing the line where his hips disappeared under his pants. He spread his hands over her lower back, caressing her curves. His hands rose; one thumb brushed over her breast. Abigail trembled.

He broke the kiss and stared down at her, the shifting colors of his eyes almost lost in the black depths of his pupils. "I wish I'd been here for Halloween," he breathed, raising one hand to brush her neckline. It was daring— too daring for a family gift store, really— swooping deep to reveal a dramatic sweep of cleavage. His fingertips brushed the lacy fabric, agonizingly close to her bare skin.

His fingers explored further, ghosting around the back of her dress. His breathing became impatient, and then he groaned and rested his forehead against hers. "How does it come off?" he asked, defeat mingling with frustration in his voice.

"Wow, a real romantic, aren't you?" Abigail couldn't help the grin that spread across her face. She directed his hand to the zip under her armpit. Really, he didn't even know that some women's dresses zipped at the side? But he was so *good* at kissing… it didn't add up. And it didn't matter. She stopped even trying to calculate.

Jasper unzipped her slowly, tenderly, as though she was the most precious and delicate thing in the world. He kissed every inch of skin he uncovered:

her shoulders as the dress's lacy arms slipped down, her breasts, her nipples—

"God, sorry," she muttered as his lips pressed against her Spanx. "That's, uh. That's so not sexy."

She pulled away, already trying to tug the supportive underwear down before he could get a good look. It wasn't that she was ashamed of her body, it was just that… well, it didn't fit very well in any of her work uniforms. It needed to be squeezed into shape. *Like a sausage,* she thought, and her shoulders slumped.

"Let me."

Jasper fell to his knees in front of her. Abigail couldn't be self-conscious in the face of his tenderness. He rolled the underwear down over her belly and hips, kissing and caressing her until she was completely naked in front of him.

Abigail trembled. Jasper looked up at her, his eyes dark, and then smiled and dipped his head between her legs.

She almost screamed as his tongue flicked out and lapped against the hot nub of her clit. Pleasure make her hips jerk and her knees weak. He licked her again, more gently this time, and a moan escaped her lips. His fingers tightened on her thighs.

Abigail muttered something that wasn't even close to being a word and grabbed Jasper by the shoulders.

She pushed him back onto the bed. He sprawled very attractively.

"That dress was incredible," he said, his eyes black with desire, "but you look even better out of it. God, you're so gorgeous." He pushed himself up and reached for her hand, pulling her down on top of him. "So—" He kissed her hand, and moved on to her wrist, "Goddamn—" the inside of her elbow, her collarbone, "beautiful."

His lips brushed along her neck. His teeth nipped at her jawline. By the time he pulled her face down to his, she was boneless with longing. But not boneless enough that she couldn't peel off his shirt. Oh, God. His chest looked as amazing as it had felt. As for his pants…

"Jasper…" A tiny corner of her sensible side, all but drowned by desire, waved its hand. She groaned. "Oh, hell. I don't know if I've got…"

Jasper's eyes widened. "Oh. I don't—" He cleared his throat. "I wasn't exactly expecting…"

Wasn't expecting to get laid? So, what, I'm just that appealing? Abigail wasn't sure she believed it… but a tendril of warmth uncurled inside her, shining gold with satisfaction. She pushed herself up on her elbows. If neither of them had condoms, then she really should be trying to stop thinking about how amazing his chest felt against her bare breasts, her nipples pebbling against his hot skin. She definitely shouldn't be losing herself in the memory of his kisses. Or imagining how the hot, hard ridge pressing against her belly would feel in her hands… between her legs…

She squeezed her eyes shut, forcing her brain into gear. "Bathroom cabinet," she managed to spit out. "Or— emergency kit? In the kitchen…"

She did have condoms somewhere. She remembered buying them. A long, long time ago. When moving to a new town was going to mean a new life, a new, exciting Abigail.

Where had boring, dateless Abigail put them?

Jasper's eyes met hers. "Bathroom?"

"That way. I'll check the kitchen."

Abigail pulled open drawers. The first aid kit? Maybe she would have put the condoms in there? But where was it? She wracked her memory. It was *in* the kitchen, she knew— she'd had some paranoia about slicing herself open while preparing dinner. Aha!

"Dammit," she whispered as she found the bag and ripped it open. Bandages. Antiseptic. Insect repellent?

No condoms.

"Here!" Jasper called from the bathroom. She ran back to the bedroom and found him brandishing a strip of condoms like a flag.

Abigail jumped back onto the bed at the same moment he did. Her limbs tangled deliciously with his. Hot, hard, and *hers*.

Jasper kissed her. She kissed him back, eager and hot with desire.

Her fingers found the button fastening his pants. The zip. The hard, thick rod of his cock brushed against her knuckles as she pulled on the zip, and her stomach fluttered. Oh, God. She was really doing this. And she wasn't worried, or shy, or trying to hide her belly and thighs. She wanted him to touch every part of her.

She dragged his pants down and took his cock in her hands. It was hot, and hard, but soft as well, the skin delicate, his sharp intake of breath heart-achingly vulnerable as she wrapped her fingers around his length.

The tear of foil. His hand wrapped around hers, and then he pulled the condom on. Ready for her. She rolled onto her back, pulling him with her. Her legs fell apart naturally. She'd never wanted anyone as much as she wanted him, now. *Right* now.

She cupped his cheek in one hand. His eyes were flooded black, pupils blown wide and dark with lust. But there was fire there, too, and gold, colors swirling in a ring around the black. Her breath caught in her throat.

Jasper kissed her until she thought she would melt with desire. He buried one hand in her hair, the other sliding down her side to her hip. Abigail's breath stuttered as he moved on top of her.

For one heartbeat, they lay still together, Jasper's cock pressing against her entrance. He pulled his lips away from hers and gazed down at her, fingers tangling in her hair. His face was flushed, his eyes shadowed with desire. Abigail trembled with anticipation.

"Please," she whimpered, and wrapped her legs around him.

He thrust into her and it felt so good Abigail gasped. Jasper groaned as he filled her completely, their two bodies joining as one. He kissed her, and when he stopped, his eyes were blazing.

"You're amazing," he whispered, and began to slowly pump in and out of her. Sensation sparked deep inside her, every movement building the bonfire of her pleasure higher.

Jasper moved slowly, taking his time. Abigail watched his face, and the heat in his eyes made her skin tingle all over. He smiled and kissed her again, teasing her lips and then moving on to her jaw, her neck, the delicate skin under her ear…

"Tell me if you want anything else," he whispered, and Abigail had to bite her lip to stop from whimpering.

"I think if you went any faster, I'd explode," she admitted. Jasper's slow, careful lovemaking was the most intense she'd ever experienced. It was so… intimate. She'd been so eager for him— and she didn't want it to be over yet.

"Hmm." Jasper's chuckle vibrated against her neck. "I'd better slow down, then. I want to enjoy every inch of you."

Goosebumps broke out on the backs of Abigail's arms as his eyes caught hers. He buried himself inside her again, slowly, God, so slowly— and then he was trailing kisses down her collarbone, onto her breasts.

He took her nipple in his mouth and swirled his tongue around it until Abigail gasped. A bright pulse of pleasure went directly from her breast to between her legs, electric-sharp. She rolled her hips, wriggling under Jasper's weight. Oh, she wanted to take it slow, too, wanted to see what Jasper meant by *every inch*— but her body was demanding more. It wanted fireworks.

Not yet, she pleaded with herself, squeezing her eyes shut.

Mistake.

With her eyes shut, her body's other senses went into overdrive. She breathed in, and Jasper's scent filled her, soap and spices and a sweetness that made her knees tremble. She heard his every breath, and *felt* them too, felt how the muscles of his back tensed as he groaned.

And him moving inside her, slow, slow, slow. And unstoppable.

A wave of pleasure caught Abigail by surprise, sending electric warnings through her body. She moaned and pulled his face to hers. Her breath mingled with his, rougher now. His hand slipped from her hip, strong fingers gripping her thigh, pushing her leg up.

Abigail cried out as he pushed into her again. Just the slightest change in angle, her hips shifting with Jasper's thrusts, and she was lost.

Her whole body shuddered as pleasure pulsed through her. She squeezed her legs around his waist, and he pumped in and out of her, every slow thrust forcing her orgasm further. Every time she thought she'd gone over the edge, Jasper was there, teasing more pleasure from her body.

She whimpered and he kissed her, breathing in her gasps and cries until his whole body tensed. He groaned into her lips. She felt him in her core, his cock flexing and pulsing, and she was gone again, tumbling over the edge with a cry of helpless passion.

Jasper cradled her head, holding her under him. *His.* Abigail's body was limp with satisfaction, and God, everything felt so right. Her vision was hazy.

She frowned, trying to focus, and the first thing she saw was Jasper gazing back at her.

He was still deep inside her. They were both panting and sweaty, and Abigail was half convinced her body had actually disintegrated from the strength of the orgasm she'd just had.

So the sight of Jasper's eyes looking down at her, bright and multi-colored and dancing with pleasure, really shouldn't have turned her on again so quickly.

5

ABIGAIL

DECEMBER 21

FOUR DAYS UNTIL CHRISTMAS

Abigail woke up happy, and it took her a moment to remember why. After all, it was only a few days until Christmas. Her alarm was blaring, which meant she had less than an hour to plaster on a happy face and deal with the holiday crowds at work. She should be edgy and miserable, tension twanging in her muscles before she even ventured out of bed.

Instead, her whole body was suffused with the warm glow of complete satisfaction. She smiled, her cheeks heating up as she remembered why.

Jasper.

God, he was amazing. Sexy, and funny, and sweet, and— *Really, really sexy.* He'd made good on his promise to enjoy every inch of her body the night before. They had made love over and over until they both fell asleep in each other's arms. Abigail had never been so thoroughly satisfied in her life.

She stretched out one arm. Her bed wasn't that big; he must be…

Not here.

Her eyes snapped open, proving what her questing hand had already discovered. She was alone. Just her, the tangled bedsheets, and the cold lump growing in her chest.

She sat up and wrapped her arms around herself. The happiness that had enfolded her as she woke up fell away in tatters. She felt cold, and weak, and above all, *stupid*.

What did you expect? Of course he hadn't stuck around. Why would he?

A heavy feeling settled on her limbs. For a moment, the desire to fall back into bed, cocoon herself in blankets and hide from the world was almost too strong to resist. But she had to resist it. She couldn't let herself marinate in unhappiness, not now, not this close to Christmas. She had to move.

She jumped up and hurried to the bathroom. There's no point feeling sorry for yourself, she told herself firmly as she turned on the shower. You just got laid more in one night than you have in five years. You should be happy, not moping around just because…

She sighed and hung her head under the pounding spray. Anyway, he was a great distraction, if nothing else. And late nights start tonight, so it's not like you'd have time for anything else, even if he didn't have better things to do.

By the time she got out of the shower, Abigail had almost convinced herself that she was fine. Not happy, maybe, but… fine. She wrapped a towel around herself and automatically trudged over to her clothes drying rack. She was working a double shift today so there was no point her getting dressed in normal clothes when she'd be in uniform all day—

She stopped, and swore. Her work costume wasn't hanging on the clothes rack. Because she hadn't washed it last night. Abigail pinched her nose and groaned. No, she'd left it bundled into a wet, smelly lump at the bottom of her bag, while she was busy with her *great distraction.*

Abigail glanced at the clock. Forty-five minutes before she had to be at work. *Shit.*

She yanked her wardrobe door open. Nothing that would pass muster as an elf costume, of course. But maybe there would be a spare tunic at work she could borrow. Or— she shuddered— maybe if she just wore a normal skirt and leggings, and Carol's jumper, that would be Christmassy enough for Mr. Bell…

Someone knocked at the front door. Abigail frowned. She wasn't expecting a delivery. Maybe they had the wrong place. She shook her head and sorted through her clothes. *Is blue or purple more Christmas-appropriate?* she wondered, and then grabbed a plain black skirt and a pair of thermal tights.

Whoever it was knocked again. Abigail pulled on the skirt, frowning. *Had* she ordered something? No. There was no way. She was always careful to cancel all her deliveries around Christmas, because she didn't want to wait around expecting packages that might run late, or never come.

Rat-tatta-tat!

Abigail groaned and grabbed a top. Whoever it was, they weren't giving up. And she had forty minutes to get to work. Enough time to grab a bite on the way— *not* at Gustaaf's, she really couldn't handle that right now— and get there in time to try to sweet-talk the boss into letting her get away with being out of costume…

She yanked the door open, and her mouth fell open. "Jasper?"

Jasper was standing with one hand up to knock. He was wearing the same clothes he'd had on last night, but slightly rumpled. The moment he saw her, a smile lit up his face.

Abigail stared at him. "You… you came back?"

Jasper laughed self-deprecatingly. "And got myself locked out. Here," he said, raising both hands. "Breakfast. Coffee. And your elf costume, freshly laundered. I woke up early, so I thought I might as well make myself useful."

"I— you—" Abigail swallowed hard. "Uh, you better come in. You brought food? *Definitely* come in."

She stepped back, feeling dazed. He had come back. There he was, knocking snow off his shoes before he came indoors. Hanging up his coat. In her apartment.

Reaching out to tip her head back, and kissing her, in her apartment. Abigail's whole body flushed with delight and surprise.

"I can't believe you did my laundry," she muttered as he handed her the garment bag.

He grinned. "Well, I figured it was my fault you didn't have a chance to get everything sorted last night. I got them to do the stockings, too, I didn't know if you'd have spares or not."

Nope, candy-cane leggings are not a part of my normal wardrobe, Abigail thought. She glanced at the clock. Thirty-five minutes. *Shoot.* "Thank you so much."

"Save your thanks for when you see what I bought for breakfast." He set a paper bag on her kitchen bench and Abigail grabbed plates.

Thirty-three minutes. *Oh, why the hell did I sign up for double shifts?*

Jasper grinned at her. "Thankfully, Cole wasn't around to sabotage things this time, but you know, we are related. It might run in the family." He unfolded the top of the bag and the delicious smell of warm, fresh baking wafted out. "Voila!"

"That smells amazing." Abigail inhaled deeply. "I'm not getting any traces of orange, or mint… that's a good sign."

"Nope. Traditional, long-tested flavor combinations only." Jasper paused, his eyes flicking to hers. "Er, I got them to do them fresh, without any of the icing decorations…"

He tipped a pile of breakfast muffins onto the plates. Abigail recognized them: the bakery a few streets away sold them. She would have grabbed one on her way to work. But she would have had to choose between muffins decorated with piped-icing snowmen, trees, and Santa hats. These ones were plain.

"Thanks." She was so surprised, she couldn't stop the smile that stole over her face. She ducked her head, feeling like an idiot, and grabbed a cheddar and chives muffin. Her favorite. Especially when she didn't have to bite through a grinning snowman to get at the good stuff. "For the drycleaning, and getting breakfast, and… well, putting up with my stupid Christmas thing…" She stuffed the muffin in her mouth to stop herself from talking.

Jasper's eyes danced as he grabbed a pumpkin and cream cheese muffin. "Honestly, sugar icing on savory muffins? I don't know what they were thinking."

Abigail swallowed. "Well, you know this town. Everyone goes crazy over Christmas."

"Which does make me wonder what a person who hates Christmas is doing, living here." Jasper's eyes went wide. "Er, I mean that in a non-judgmental way…"

Abigail waved his apologies away. "No, it's all right." She took another bite of muffin. It really was good. "I moved here a few years ago. Grew up back in the city, but after Mom died, I wanted a change. I'd always loved mountains, so I packed up and moved here one spring… and didn't realize what I had gotten myself into until the decorations started going up. In August."

"You didn't want to move back?"

Abigail shrugged. "Sure, maybe after another few years of double shifts I'll be able to afford it." She laughed. "It's not so bad the rest of the year, though. I still like the mountains. Just have to tunnel-vision my way through the holidays."

"You work at a gift shop. That must require a bit more than tunnel vision." Jasper brushed crumbs off his fingers onto the plate. "Creamer in your coffee?"

"Please. And who needs tunnel vision when I have that stupid hat falling over my eyes at work all day? Speaking of…" She glanced at the clock and swore. Surely they hadn't been talking that long? "I have to get to work. My shift starts in ten minutes, and Mr. Bell is a stickler for punctuality. In fact, according to him, I'm already late…"

She ripped her elf outfit out of the garment bag and hesitated. Yes, Jasper had already seen her naked. But it still felt weird to undress in front of him.

Her lips tingled where he'd kissed her hello.

Yeah, taking your clothes off in front of him when you're already late to work is a terrible idea, she decided, and darted into the bathroom.

Jasper had tidied up their breakfast by the time she came out again. He handed her a takeaway cup of coffee as she checked the clock. "Three minutes. Think we can make it?"

She stared at him. "You're not coming to work with me."

"Aren't I?" He linked his arm through hers. "When else will be get a chance to plan our next date?"

"Our next— ?" Abigail's eyes flicked to the clock. *No time.* "Fine. Let's go."

6

JASPER

Abigail was marching at top speed down the street, and Jasper couldn't decide which he would prefer: marching arm-in-arm with her, or following a few paces behind and enjoying the sight of her candy-cane legs. Her elf dress was shorter than her coat, giving the appealing illusion that all she had on under her quilted winter jacket was the stockings.

He decided to stick with marching arm-in-arm. She was walking so fast he was worried she'd leave him in the dust if he let go. She'd raced around the apartment before they left, stuffing a few things furtively in a bag, and now she was practically sprinting down the street. If he let go and she left him behind, he'd never get their plans sorted.

The clock was ticking. He hadn't felt the strange, sick shaking apart of his human and dragon halves since he first kissed Abigail— but he knew he wasn't home safe yet. Tick, tock.

"Four days," he muttered out loud.

"What?"

Damn it. "Uh, I was just thinking. Four days until Christmas. That gives me…" He made a show of counting on the fingers of his free hand. "Hmm… twenty-four hours in a day, minus, I'm assuming, eight-hour work days— I guess we'll need to sleep a bit, too, let's say seven hours a night although I don't think we quite managed that last night… I make it thirty-six hours available for dating." He lowered his head to whisper in her ear: "Not including the hours where you're sleeping in my arms."

A line formed between her eyebrows. "Less than that."

He stared at her, and she grimaced. "Sorry. I'm working double shifts."

"Lunch break?" he suggested. She shook her head.

"The shifts are back-to-back, so I don't get a long break between them. Just a half-hour lunch. At three. *If* we're not slammed, which… we're a Christmas gift store. We've been slammed since Halloween." She rubbed her forehead and frowned harder. "We're meant to get a short break for dinner too, but… well, *meant to* doesn't always line up with reality. So that's, what… sixteen hours?"

"Damn it, and I'm meant to look after Cole from two while his mom gets the Santa presents." Jasper tried to smile, though his mind was still screaming in disbelief. Sixteen hours?

He shook himself. Sixteen hours into four made four hours a day for him to woo her. He'd follow her around carrying her grocery shopping, if that was what it took. Date nights at the laundromat. Or, at the very least:

"Dinner tonight?"

She grimaced. "I don't get off until ten again."

"You're kidding me!"

Abigail let out a bark of laughter. "Afraid not. I'm on late nights until Christmas Eve—"

"Great, so—"

"— When I get off whenever Mr. Bell decides the shop is going to close, and no earlier. Sorry." She bit her lip. "I didn't exactly plan out my week on the understanding I'd be spending time with anyone."

Jasper's heart twisted. Her tone was ironic, but— She really doesn't have anyone to spend Christmas with?

"I don't see why that rules out dinner," he said out loud.

Abigail raised one eyebrow. "Mini pancakes and apple tart again?" She wasn't quite smiling; he couldn't read the expression on her face. Whatever it was, it looked precarious, like she was standing on the edge of a cliff waiting for his next words.

"I'll think of something even better." A plan was beginning to formulate in his head. She said she liked mountains… And now she was smiling again.

Properly. Jason's dragon preened smugly as they turned the corner into the square. "Here we are."

They came to a dead stop outside Abigail's work. Abigail turned to him. Her face was flushed with exertion. He couldn't help but think of how she'd looked the night before, her eyes shining with pleasure as she moved beneath him.

God, he wished he could take her away, right now. Inside him, his dragon flapped its wings. *Fly away with her?*

Maybe in a few days.

"I'll see you tonight," he promised. "Ten o'clock, right outside this door."

"Mmm," Abigail said non-commitally. "All right. If you insist." She turned to open the door— then spun back around and pulled him into a kiss. "You had *better* be here," she whispered into his ear, and then fled.

Jasper watched her disappear into the back of the shop. Joy glowed inside him like a sun, warming him from head to toe. Of course he would be here when she got off her shift. He loved her. He loved her!

And his dragon would love her, too. Once it met her properly, not just seeing her through his human eyes. Everything would be perfect. He turned around, looking across at the giant Christmas tree he'd been standing under when he first saw her.

This was going to be the most perfect Christmas ever.

His pocket buzzed and he pulled out his phone. "Opal! Merry Christmas, best and most wonderful of sisters."

Her snort crackled through the speaker. "Hey, bro. I couldn't help but notice our guest bed looks remarkably un-slept-in this morning. And you didn't pick up the key for the cottage, which I thought you might do, so… Things go well with the roof lady?"

"Her name is Abigail. And she's…" His voice trailed off. There were too many words he could use to describe her— *wonderful, incredible, heart-stoppingly gorgeous*— and none of them were enough. He sighed, looking up at the strings of Christmas lights hanging above the square.

"Oh, it's like that, is it?" Opal laughed fondly. "I'm happy for you, Jas. Actually, I'm fucking relieved. You were cutting it kind of close, there. So, are you bringing her up to the lodge?"

Jasper kicked at a snow-drift, breaking through the crust of ice that had formed overnight. "Hmm."

"Jas?" Opal's voice held a note of warning.

"She has to work. I'm seeing her again tonight, but she doesn't get off until late and… I don't want to disturb everyone once you're already gotten Cole to bed."

Opal gave a disbelieving snort. "You haven't sealed the deal yet, have you?"

"Christ, sis, way to take the romance out of it." Jasper breathed in. The square smelled like spices, and coffee, and— well, not pine, actually. The giant tree was plastic, after all. "She's human. It's not like with you and Hank."

"Worried you'll scare her off?"

"Worried she'll think she cracked her head open when she fell off the roof and got a concussion, sure." Jasper's heart flipped. How would Abigail react when she saw his dragon?

If she ever does, whispered a quiet voice in his head. His skin went cold.

Of course she would see his dragon. Before Christmas. And after Christmas. And every Christmas afterwards. She was his mate. She completed him.

His skin prickled as he realized the absolute truth of that statement. With her in his life, he would be whole. He wasn't going to lose half of himself.

And what if you can't make her fall in love with you by your birthday?

He shook his head. That wasn't going to happen. He had a plan. Four days of perfect dates, and then she would be his.

"You're still looking after Cole this afternoon, right?" Opal's voice cut through his thoughts.

"Wouldn't miss it."

"Oh, and you're still in town, right? Can you pick me up a few things before you head back to the lodge?"

Jas listened as Opal began to recite her shopping list, but quickly gave up and grabbed a pen and paper from his coat pocket. He was going to need to go all over town to pick up everything she wanted. Which would mean getting a rental.

Which was perfect, actually. It would give him a chance to organize some things. And pick up a few items of his own…

Jasper tipped his head back, enjoying the crisp breeze playing over his face. It was another clear night. Here in the square, the only lights in the sky were the strings of Christmas lights— and the glowing, glittering Christmas tree. But beyond the electric lights, the sky was clear, and beyond the town…

"You're here!"

Jasper spun around at Abigail's voice.

Abigail hurried up to him, her face tight with the sort of contorted half-smile people get when they're trying to hide how pleased they are. She slowed down a few paces away, and Jasper pulled her into a kiss.

"How was your day?"

"*Long.*" She breathed out heavily and rested her head against his shoulder, just for a minute. "So—you're here! What's the plan?"

Jasper rubbed his gloved hands together. Abigail's hands, he noticed, were still bare. But her legs…

"Enjoying the view?"

Jasper snapped his eyes back up to Abigail's face. Her cheeks were pink, but she was smirking. She had changed out of her candy-stripe stockings, but the black pants she was wearing instead were tightly fitting enough to capture Jasper's attention. Really, if their skin-tightness was any indication, they probably didn't provide much more insulation than the stockings...

"Because, really, if your big plan is just to stare at my legs—"

Jasper hauled his eyes up again. Abigail's cheeks were even more pink— and she looked even more pleased. "It's part of the plan, but not the whole plan." Jasper slipped his arm around her waist. With two layers of bulky winter coats between them, he couldn't feel much more than the outline of her body— but there would be time for that later. "The other part of the plan is… you said you like the mountains, right?"

"Yes…" Abigail sounded uncertain, like she was waiting for the rug to be pulled from under her feet.

Jasper reached into his pocket and pulled out a small package. It was *not* gift-wrapped— well, it was, but only in plain tissue. No Christmas wrapping paper. No ribbons, no card.

"Here. You'll need these."

Jasper rocked on the balls of his feet as Abigail slowly unwrapped the gift. His dragon watched through his eyes, unblinking.

"This is…" Abigail pulled Jasper's gift out of the tissue paper. A pair of dove-grey leather gloves, and a matching woolen scarf. She stroked the soft wool, and then looked up at Jasper, her eyebrows drawing together. "These are— thank you. They're lovely."

"I noticed you didn't have gloves on last night or this morning." Jasper's heart felt like it was about to burst. *She likes them! She accepted my gift!*

"I did have some, but I think they fell out of my pocket a few days ago— I meant to get some more at the grocery store, but these are… these are wonderful." She turned one glove inside-out, feeling the cashmere lining. Her eyes widened, and for a moment, Jasper's warm glow of success faded.

Are they too much? He'd bought them from a local designer store. They had been expensive, yes, but he couldn't possibly have bought his mate anything but the best.

Abigail closed her hands around the gloves and scarf and smiled up at him. "Thank you."

Yes!

"Great! You'd better put them on now. Tonight's date is a Chr— a winter wonderland adventure." Abigail raised one eyebrow, and he added quickly: "With dinner first."

Abigail grinned and shook her head. "All right, then. Lead on."

Jasper had been very organized: they ate at a small deli that specialized in magnificent platters of cheese and meats, and crunchy fresh-baked bread. Then it was back out into the chilly winter night, and the next step in their adventure.

Their first stop was the rental car Jasper had picked up that morning. Swinging into town on a bus was fine when you were planning to spend the week out in the lodge, with the family 4WD— not so much when it came to wining and dining a beautiful lady. The rental was sleek, red with gold highlights. Jasper glanced sideways at Abigail as he opened the door for her, trying to gauge her reaction.

Red and gold were just colors, after all. They weren't necessarily *Christmassy* colors. And she still looked happy. *So far, so good.*

Abigail smiled at him as he sat down and pulled on his seatbelt. "So, where are we— *ooh,*" she said, wriggling slightly. "Are these… heated seats? Oh, my God. You could tell me we're spending the evening sitting right here, and I'd be happy."

"Sorry to disappoint," Jasper said, laughing. "I have a bit more than that planned…"

It wasn't a long drive; their destination was just at the edge of town. "Here we are," Jasper said as they rounded the final corner. He parked and turned a woebegone expression on her. "Unless you'd prefer to stay here with the car seats…"

"I haven't done this for *years*," Abigail complained, wobbling on her skates. "So if I fall over, don't blame— eek!"

She clutched at Jasper as another ice-skater sped by. Jasper wound one arm around her waist. They were at the outdoor ice rink at the edge of town. The oval-shaped rink was edged on one side by pine trees, and the other looked out down the side of the mountain.

Its exposed situation meant that the owners had gone easy on the Christmas decorations— they didn't want them blowing away into the sky— and the rink was far enough from the town itself that the ever-present Christmas carols were barely a whisper on the air.

Jasper was sure Abigail was going to love it. Even if right now she was wobbling like a new-born fawn.

"Don't worry," he said, striking a noble pose. "If you do fall, I'll be there for you to fall on top of—"

Abigail snorted and poked him in the ribs, but her eyes were shining. "Clutching your broken ribs, and groaning, *Oh, if only I'd decided to just have a quiet evening in the car with the heated seats…*"

"Save your I-told-you-so's for *after* I've been grievously injured, please." Jasper tucked the corner of Abigail's scarf back under her coat collar. "Now…"

He took her hand and skated around in front of her, until they were standing face-to-face. One hand on her waist, he took a slow, gliding step backwards. "Just relax. Move with me."

Abigail's expression was caught between aggravation and anxiety. She took a deep breath. "Okay. Move with you. You make it sound so easy, but I warn you, I was never good at this even when I was a kid…"

He stared deep into her eyes, letting his own gaze grow warm and intimate. "But this time, you're skating with me."

Her cheeks went pink. "And that's going to make a difference, is it?"

"Of course it is." He pulled her close and whispered into her ear: "Because you've never been skating before with someone who knows your body like I do."

Hot breath blasted his neck as she gasped in surprise. "You—"

Jasper glided backwards, drawing her with him. At first she stiffened and he changed his weight to counterbalance her— and then she relaxed, limbs becoming loose and they moved together, bodies in sync as they slid across the ice.

"Oh my God," Abigail gasped. Jasper spun around, linking arms with her to skate side-by-side across the rink. Her arm went stiff as iron. "No, please, go back—"

He obeyed and she grimaced at him ruefully. Her cheeks were pink.

"Sorry— I didn't mean to freak out—" She groaned, her eyes slipping down. "I just see everyone else going so *fast* and I'm sure I'm going to skate straight into them…"

"You think I'd let you do that?" Jasper squeezed her hand.

She groaned. "I think the sheer *magnitude* of my incompetence would send me barreling into them regardless of how hard you tried to stop me."

"Whereas if I'm in front of you… out of sight, out of mind?"

"You're nicer scenery, anyway." She grinned and Jasper laughed.

"Always happy to be useful."

Jasper reached out with his shifter senses. His dragon complied happily, sharpening his hearing and awareness of his physical surroundings. Using his shifter senses in his human form felt strange, like stretching a muscle that didn't exist— but it was effective. Jasper skated backwards around the rink, magically avoiding every other skater.

With his other senses on high alert, his eyes were free to drown in Abigail's gaze. Her expression was open, clear and *happy*, without a trace of the previous night's wary defenses. Jasper realized, smugly, that she must be so focused on skating that she didn't have any attention left for the spiky walls she'd carefully built around herself.

"Enjoying yourself?"

Her eyes flicked to his, bright as stars. "Maybe. Oh, hell— *yes*. I never thought I would enjoy ice-skating this much!"

He pulled her into a slow spin, drawing her under a pine tree at the edge of the rink. "Here. Put your hand on the railing."

"Why?"

He pulled her scarf down over her chin. "Because I'm going to kiss you, and I don't want you to fall over."

Abigail's eyes softened as Jasper pulled her to his chest and bent his head to kiss her. Her lips were soft, and warm from being covered by her scarf. Her nose, not so much.

She giggled as he kissed the tip of her nose. "Hey!"

"You're cold. It's my job to warm you up." He kissed her nose again, holding her tight at she squirmed. "And to stop you from falling over…"

Abigail' shoulders shook as she pulled her face away and burrowed it into his own scarf. She let out a deep contented breath. "There. That's better. Warm, and no tickling."

She molded her body against his. He couldn't feel her warmth through all their clothes, but he could feel the shape of her, her curves and softness— and the steely spine that was starting to unbend for him. He ran his gloved hand down her back and she sighed happily.

Happiness opened like a spring blossom in his heart. So what if he was on a deadline? There was still time for moments like this. There *had* to be time for moments like this. Quiet, perfect togetherness.

Inside him, his dragon resettled its wings. Here under the stars, with the night air still and crisp around them— perfect moment or not, it wanted more. And Jasper knew just what to do.

He unwound his arms from around Abigail and took her hands. "Ready for another spin?" he asked, quirking one eyebrow up. Her eyes shone and she started to move aside so that he could take up his place facing her again.

Jasper put his hands on her shoulders, stopping her. "No— I have something else in mind."

Abigail's eyebrows shot up. "O-kayyy…" Her uncertainty was clear, but so was her determination not to back down. "What's your plan to stop me from crashing into all the other skaters?"

"This." Jasper took her hand and skated behind her so he could gently cover her eyes with his other hand. He whispered into her ear. "Do you trust me?"

"Yes," Abigail breathed, and then caught her breath. "I… yes. I do." She laughed at herself. "Well, I trust you to do *this*, at least. God knows why. I'm probably going to wake up in the hospital."

"Nonsense. Pine Valley doesn't have a hospital." Jasper snuck a kiss from Abigail as she groaned, and then straightened up. "Let's go."

Jasper skated forward slowly, his own momentum pushing Abigail along. They were close enough that he could feel her body's reactions: her brief moment of tension as she began to move blindly across the ice, and the calmness that flooded through her body as she got into the rhythm. Skate, and glide. Skate, and glide. Two bodies, moving together. Jasper and his mate.

Just as we should be, he thought.

His dragon senses let him avoid the other skaters. He led Abigail around them, sweeping past meandering couples, parents each holding one of their tiny offspring's hands, and giggling clusters of teenagers. The speedster who had almost made Abigail lose her footing earlier whipped past again, so fast Jasper could feel the wind of his wake on his cheeks. Which meant Abigail must have felt it too— but she hadn't tensed, or lost her balance.

She trusted him. She might have walked it back before, specified that she trusted him *to do this*… but those weren't the words that had sprung instinctively from her lips. She trusted him.

And the ice ahead of them was empty. And his dragon was stretching its wings inside him.

"Want to go faster?" he asked.

Abigail squeezed his hand. "Yes!"

He slipped his hand from hers and held on to her waist, keeping his other hand over her eyes. Her breaths came faster. He thought if he took off his glove, wormed his hand down under her collar, under her scarf, her pulse would beat like a hummingbird's wings under his fingertips.

He left his hands where they were— gloves on, clothing undisturbed— and started to move. Slowly at first, and then faster, until the ice flew past under his skates. And Abigail kept pace, throwing herself blindly into the night, trusting that she was safe in his arms.

The speedster zipped past again. Jasper barely noticed. They were approaching the far side of the rink, where the mountain fell away in a vista of snow and rock and starry night sky.

Jasper pulled Abigail into a spin. He grabbed both her hands, uncovering her eyes— but she kept them shut, her head flung up to the sky.

They spun together across the ice, Jasper carefully balancing Abigail's weight, holding her safe in their own private world. The other skaters were staying close to the trees; they were the only two venturing out to the far edge, where the world dropped away. Where they could almost be flying.

Jasper drew Abigail closer, slowing them down as they approached the edge. She was still squeezing her eyes shut, but her mouth was stretched into a delighted grin. As they came to a stop, Jasper couldn't help bending down to kiss her.

She opened her eyes as he pulled back and then grabbed his collar, kissing him back so passionately it left them both breathless.

"That was incredible," she gasped, her words bubbling against his lips. "It was like— it was like *flying*. Like we were flying across the ice…"

She abandoned the sentence and kissed him again. Jasper's heart leapt. Like flying? *If she thought that was incredible, she's going to* love *real flying,* he thought.

He slipped his arm around her waist and led her slowly to the railing around the edge of the rink, out of the way of any other skaters who ventured this far from the hot-drinks-and-cookies stands. Abigail stood facing the railing, looking out across the immense, dark vista of the snow-covered mountains. Jasper fitted himself against her back, sneaking a kiss along the curve of her jaw.

"It's beautiful out here," Abigail whispered.

Jasper nuzzled under her scarf for another kiss. "Of course it's beautiful. It's your home. It's got a lot to live up to."

Abigail ducked her head and snorted. "Oh, come on… I can't believe I've never been out here before."

"And you've lived here how long?" The words were out before Jasper could stop them. But Abigail just sighed.

"I don't get out much at this time of year. Not normally." She glanced up at him, one corner of her mouth curling up. "Not without anyone to drag me out, anyway."

"Happy to be of service, ma'am," Jasper said seriously, and nipped the tip of Abigail's nose. She laughed and turned around, burying her face in his woolly scarf. "Happy to drag you anywhere you like," he added, and was rewarded with a snort and a giggle.

Abigail sighed happily, and murmured something into his neck. Her voice was muffled by his scarf, and he couldn't make out the words.

"Hmm?" He pressed a kiss against her cheek and she tipped her head up. Her eyes reflected the lights strung over the rink, shining like stars. A shy smile hovered around her lips.

"Jasper," she said quietly, "I—"

A whoop echoed across the ice. Abigail twisted to look past Jasper and he followed her gaze: two vans had just pulled up in the car lot and were spilling festively-dressed partygoers out into the calm night. Jasper could see their excited grins from where he and Abigail were standing— and their corny Christmas sweaters, and their elf hats and candy-striped scarves. And he could definitely hear the cheerful carols blaring from the vans' speakers.

Abigail sagged into him. "Huh," she muttered flatly, and then shook herself. "What do you think— tourist group, or a work party? Those outfits look like they came from the same wholesaler Mr. Bell got our uniforms from."

She was still smiling, but it was a sharp, brittle smile. Jasper wound his arm more firmly around her waist. "Well, they all look pretty alike," he said, taking up the game. "Maybe one huge, extended family, out for some Christmas fun?"

Abigail's waist stiffened under his hand. Her smile was frozen on her face, so brittle it looked about to crack.

Last night, her disdain for Christmas had been a hot anger. It had stung at the time, but he preferred it to this flash of vulnerability.

Jasper pulled her close automatically, his dragon rising up inside him. He wanted to wrap his wings around her like a cloak and fly away with her, take her away from whatever it was that had made her freeze up like that.

She pressed her face into his chest. He thought he heard her swear softly, and when she lifted her head again, she looked… fine.

At least, she looked like someone who was trying very hard to look fine. She was smiling, but the corners of her mouth were tight, and her eyes weren't sparkling anymore.

"Hey," Jasper murmured, his stomach clenching. "Is everything okay?"

"Yeah, it's just…" Abigail shrugged tightly. "It's nothing."

Across the ice rink, the last bars of Jingle Bells faded away, and were immediately followed by *I Saw Mommy Kissing Santa Claus*. A ragged cheer burst out of the office holiday party/family reunion group, and several of them joined in with the song.

They were all off-tune— *and* all off-tune in different ways, which was impressive— but Jasper's heart still warmed at the sound of people cheerfully caroling each other. *That* was what Christmas was about. People relaxing with each other. Letting loose. Celebrating.

He looked down at Abigail and his stomach twisted. She was pale, and however much effort it was taking her to look like she was fine, the cracks were starting to show.

"You want to get out of here?" Jasper suggested, and her smile flashed, genuine and surprised.

"God yes." She grabbed hold of his collar. "Drag me away to somewhere you can kiss me until I fall over."

7

ABIGAIL

Abigail snuggled into the heated car seat. It was the sort of luxury she'd never imagined it— and if she was being honest, if she *had* imagined it, she probably would have told herself she would hate it. That shelling out for heated car seats was silly, and frivolous, and—

Cozy and wonderful and the best thing ever, after freezing my ass off on the ice rink. She let out a contented sigh. It was all Jasper. Without him, she would be stuck in her apartment, stubbornly eating microwave dinners and only going outside to work. Turning off the radio and TV at the wall. Staring at the sidewalk everywhere she went, just to avoid seeing anyone else actually *enjoying* the holiday season.

That was why she worked at the shop. Jasper probably thought she was crazy, hating Christmas and working at a Christmas gift store— but if he knew the truth, he'd think she was worse than crazy. The truth was, the only reason she could stand that place was because of how awful people were when they were doing their Christmas shopping. At least if some guy in a blinking-LED Christmas sweater was raging at her about missing out on the latest trendy knick-knack, she could convince herself that she wasn't the only person who found Christmas a grinding, painful chore.

Like those ice-skaters who turned up just *at the wrong moment*, she thought, and immediately shook her head. No. That wasn't fair. She might be a Grinch, but that was no reason to be nasty. The carol-singing idiots might have looked like they'd been dragged backwards through a Christmas tree, but they weren't miserable. No one who actually hated Christmas could sing carols with such reckless, tuneless abandon.

No. They were happy, and Jasper had been happy, and she was just a miserable, soulless Grinch. She hadn't even properly thanked Jasper for the scarf and gloves, even though they were the best present anyone had ever given her.

Oh, God, definitely don't tell him that. That's like, one step above socks being the most exciting Christmas present ever. One hundred percent pathetic.

She stared out the car window, blinking hard. Her eyes cleared and she realized where they were. "We're going back to my place?"

Jasper pulled in to park. "We could go back to mine, but you wouldn't come back anytime soon." He yanked on the hand brake and winced. "Let's pretend that didn't come out sounding all serial-killer. I mean, I'm staying halfway up the mountain. You can see what would happen. We get out there, it snows overnight, roads closed— or maybe I just tell you the roads are closed, because once I have you in my bed I never want to let you go."

"Hmm." Abigail rolled her eyes at him. "And then I miss work— get fired— lose my apartment, and freeze on the streets?"

"No." Jasper leaned across to kiss her. "Because you're still in my bed, remember? In this entirely theoretical situation."

"Tempting… but I'd better not risk it. Not even an avalanche could keep Mr. Bell from rocking up to yell at me for missing my shift, and if I'm living in your bed by this point, that could get embarrassing."

Jasper sighed dramatically. "There goes my plan to carry you off into the mountains."

Abigail laughed. She hadn't felt this happy in— too long. And nothing had ever been able to pull her out of her Christmas-time unhappiness as well as a single smile from Jasper could.

Warmth unspooled inside her as she undid her seatbelt. Quick as a flash, Jasper was out of the car and racing around to open the passenger door for her.

She stepped onto the sidewalk, icy air biting at her cheeks. "Aren't you staying with your family, anyway? Didn't you say something about a nephew?"

"I—" Jasper's mouth snapped shut. "Well, yes. There's the lodge. But I have my own, personal bachelor pad on the property. Believe me, I'm not going to whisk you away to a romantic snowy realm where you get woken every morning by a four-year-old dra— menace jumping on the bed."

Abigail tipped her head on one side. *Another* smile was pulling at her lips. Hadn't she run through her quota for the month already? And yet every time she looked at him, there another one was. It was almost like the guy made her happy, or something. *Almost like you might be falling—*

Her heart leapt— and she caught it and wrestled it to the ground. He was fun. And spending time with him was definitely preferable to sulking around in her apartment all alone.

"So," she said, sneaking her hand into his. "Is this some sort of hint? All this talk about trapping me in your bed… Are you suggesting I should trap *you* in *my* bed, or something?" She checked the car clock. "For the next seven hours, at least."

"Is that a promise?" Jasper smiled wickedly at her.

"When you promised to trap me in your bed, I assumed you'd be in it, too," came Jasper's plaintive voice from the bedroom.

"In a minute!" Abigail bundled her uniform into her mini washer-dryer. "I have to get the washing on!"

"I can take them to the laundromat again in the morning," Jasper argued.

"Waste of money," Abigail muttered. "Where's the laundry detergent— aha." She checked the inlet hose was firmly attached to the faucet, and dropped the drain hose into the shower. She gave the machine one last tap before she turned it on.

"Please don't flood the bathroom again," she whispered.

The little washer-dryer was a lifesaver. Her apartment building didn't have a laundry, and the laundromat around the corner mostly catered for wealthy tourists— with prices to match. One more thing she hadn't taken into account when she moved here.

If only the machine didn't break down and flood the bathroom one time out of ten. She'd bought it for herself a few Christmases ago, which had been a mistake. It was stupid to think that if she'd bought it any other time of year, it would have crapped out less, but… well. Abigail and Christmas had never mixed.

A black-button eye caught hers as she stopped at the door to turn off the bathroom light. Her stomach twisted. The kitten toy from the shop roof was hanging from the shower head, where she'd left it to drip dry. It had dripped, but it didn't look like it would be dry anytime soon.

"Why didn't I just throw you out?" she muttered, and closed the shower door.

Jasper was waiting for her in the bedroom. In her bed. Completely naked, complete with cunningly placed pillow and a reproachful look in his eyes.

"Don't look at me like that. I can't abandon my chores *every* night," Abigail said. A mischievous impulse made her grin. "Speaking of chores, there really are a few other things I need to get done…"

"Please, have mercy!" Jasper leapt from the bed and knelt at her feet. "Whatever it is, leave me to do it when you go to work tomorrow. Vacuuming. Dishes. Polishing the silverware."

"Aha!" Abigail cried, arching one eyebrow. "So that's it, is it? Your dastardly plan. Trick your way into my bed and my apartment, and then run off with the silver while my back is turned." She ran her toes along Jasper's thigh, stopping just short of the still-intact modesty pillow. "Joke's on you, it's all aluminum. And plastic."

Jasper groaned and let his head fall back. Abigail's eyelids lowered as she looked down his body, her gaze trailing slowly from his neck, to the curve of his collarbone— down to his firm pectorals and the flat planes of his stomach and abs, the deep, alluring V that led between his legs…

Abigail lifted her eyes again to find Jasper staring straight at her, a smirk hovering on his lips. "Damn it, you've found me out," he murmured, his voice like honey-smooth chocolate. "If only I could think of a way to distract you from my nefarious, cutlery-thieving ways…"

The pillow slipped lower. Abigail licked her lips.

"Go on…" she said, sinking down in front of him. "Distract me."

8

JASPER

DECEMBER 22

THREE DAYS BEFORE CHRISTMAS

Jasper parked around the corner from the square— a cause for celebration, given how busy the town center was this close to Christmas. Gold and red lights glimmered above the street, leading towards the square. Towards his Abigail.

He turned the engine off and closed his eyes, just for a moment. *Abigail.* Letting her leave the bed this morning had been almost impossible. Seeing her dress for work— he'd wanted to shift then and there, pick her up and fly her deep into the mountains, to the Heartwell lodge and his personal hoard.

A shiver ran through him. His hoard. He would take her there, eventually. *Eventually? Try sometime in the next couple of days.* And when he did…

Jasper frowned. Abigail was so prickly about the magic of Christmas, and he was beginning to suspect there was more to it than just grumpy Grinch-ness. The look on her face the night before… He shook himself. How would she react to him inviting her to join with him on top of a pile of gold?

Guess we'll find out soon. He had plans for tonight: romantic, non-Christmassy, perfect plans. If everything went well, the night would end with Abigail in his arms, and on his hoard. And then his prickly, sharp, glorious Abigail would truly be his mate, now and forever.

He jumped out of the car, leaping over a pile of icy snow. Inside him, his dragon rose up, wings outstretched. *Fly!*

Not yet, he reminded it. Didn't we fly enough this morning, with Cole? Not that what he does can really be called "flying"… more "falling with intent"… Intent of dive-bombing, most of the time.

Heart light, he practically skipped down the street, buoyed by the glow of festive lights and the enticing scents of spice and coffee on the air. *The only way this evening could be better was if I could smell snow on the air, as well,* he thought, kicking at a small snow-drift as he rounded the corner into the square. Clearly it *had* snowed in Pine Valley recently, probably only just before he arrived. It would be a white Christmas. But that wasn't the same as seeing snowflakes settle on his mate's eyelashes, and kissing them off her lips…

When she is *your mate*, he reminded himself. When he'd made things *official*. Yes. When he'd completed the simple task of revealing his true nature to her, and convincing her they were meant to be together, and taking her up the mountain—

His foot slipped. Jasper shifted his weight to keep his balance, but his legs didn't obey. For a moment, his vision swam, going double. Four legs slipped out from under him. Two wearing dark trousers, and two huge and scaled.

Jasper squeezed his eyes shut. When he looked down at himself again, there were only two legs. Human. Wearing pants. And one human ass, currently soaking up snowmelt from the sidewalk.

He groaned and rolled onto his knees. His vision swam again and he pinched the bridge of his nose. He might not be able to *see* his dragon's phantom body any more, but he could feel…

A shiver jolted down his spine. He could feel his dragon, but not like he ever had before. It had always been a part of him. When he was human-shaped, the dragon curled up in the fire of his soul, deep inside. And when he was dragon-shaped, his human side made itself at home in the dragon's fiery heart. But now— it was like the dragon was being shaken loose. Like something was tearing it out of him.

He was losing his dragon.

No! It's too soon! He gritted his teeth and *pulled*, wrapping psychic arms around the burning shape of his dragon as tremors struck them both. *I still have three days— not now—*

"Jasper?" Abigail's voice exploded into his mind like fireworks. He took a shaky breath. The tremors stopped. His dragon was still there, safe inside him. He pushed himself up and saw Abigail running towards him. "Jasper, what happened? Are you all right?"

Jasper forced himself upright before Abigail reached him. Too fast. He swayed, and then she was with him, holding him upright.

He let his head drop onto hers and inhaled deeply. Her scent filled him, sweet and warm and *his*.

"I'm fine," he mumbled into her hair. "I fell— hit my knee. Like an idiot."

"Are you sure?" Abigail held him at arm's length, frowning as she inspected his face. "You're so pale." She bit her lip and Jasper's heart lurched. His mate might be spiny, but the spikes surrounded a soft, delicate heart. "If you want to cancel tonight—"

"Never." He tipped her head back and kissed her, tender and— he had to admit it— more than a little desperate.

Abigail's lips were warm and soft. Her touch grounded him with memories of their two nights together, and promises of more. He moaned gently into her mouth and she pressed into him, her hands gripping his coat.

"Falling over in the street is embarrassing enough," he murmured. "I don't want to go and lick my wounds at home by myself."

Abigail stilled. Jasper forced himself not to respond. Not pull away, and not pull her closer, either. After a moment she scowled and tugged at his jacket, yanking him closer to her. "I wasn't going to send you home *alone*. I meant, if you wanted a quiet evening, instead…"

He kissed her again, relief washing through him. She wasn't pushing him away. The shaking was gone. He was himself again, dragon and human and *whole*.

"There'll be time for a quiet evening later," he assured her, nipping at the fingertips of her glove. The glove *he* had given her. "First, I want to take you somewhere special."

"How far away is this 'somewhere special'?" Abigail asked. Her eyes narrowed. "This isn't you stealing me away to your mountain bachelor-pad, is it?"

"And risk Mr. Bell's wrath? Certainly not."

"So where are we going?"

Jasper shot her what he hoped was a mysterious, sexy smile. "You'll see."

Abigail mock-frowned at him and he laughed.

"Don't worry, I'll get you home in time for your beauty sleep. Not that you need it."

Abigail ducked her head, cheeks pink. "Well, I sure didn't get it last night. I was almost asleep on my feet the last few hours at work. If I have to listen to another Christmas carol tonight, I'll scream."

Jasper paused with his finger two inches from the radio button, and smoothly transitioned the gesture into reaching for Abigail's hand. She wove her fingers between his, staring out the window as they left the small town behind.

They were driving in the opposite direction to the previous night's date, deeper into the mountains instead of looking out over the foothills. Snow-covered bluffs rose either side of the road, white peaks disappearing into the darkness. The pine trees were so dark against the snow they looked like black shadows of nothingness.

"It's so beautiful out here," Abigail said quietly.

"Picture perfect. I'm not surprised the town goes crazy over Christmas, with views like this in their backyard. It's like the North Pole out here."

"Except there aren't any trees at the North Pole," Abigail said absently.

Jasper kept his eyes on the road, but his attention was laser-focused on his mate. Had she just said something Christmassy, without sounding like she hated it?

His skin prickled. His dragon was interested in what he'd just heard. *Very* interested.

Play it cool. He cleared his throat. "Well, there aren't flying reindeer, either, but it's all part of the magic, isn't it?"

She snorted, but it didn't sound like her heart was in it. "Oh, *magic*. That's one word for it, I guess. But it's all just lies people tell children, isn't it? Until they can't even be bothered with that anymore."

Not all magic is fake, Jasper wanted to say, his heart sinking. I'm not fake. What I feel for you isn't fake. But if you think Christmas is all about lying, how can I convince you that this isn't just a fling, and you're truly my soul mate?

By taking her out of her Christmas-mad town. That was his plan. He just had to hope it would work.

A few minutes later, he followed a side-road into the outskirts of the forest and pulled up outside a long, low building. It was a classic log cabin on commercial scale, with red-painted windows and a sign hanging above the entryway: *Home of the Puppy Express!*

"Oh, I've heard of this place!" Abigail leaned forward, staring at the sign. "I always wanted to give it a go, but I— um. Well. You know."

"You don't get out much this time of year, I know. It's a good thing I came along." Jasper practically skipped around the car to open the door for her. "The ideal companion for a night out."

"Or in," she murmured, leaning close to him as she got out of the car. "Brr— is this where we're having dinner? I hope it's warm inside. I'm not really dressed for it." She was wearing the same tight black pants she had worn to their date the night before, but it was even colder here under the trees than it had been at the rink.

"Not a problem." Jasper reached into the back seat and pulled out a bag. "I knew we wouldn't have time to go back to yours for a change of clothes, so I picked these up earlier. I think I've got the sizes right…"

He watched as Abigail looked inside the bag. "You— these are from the most expensive shop in town! You didn't seriously… oh, my God." She looked up at him. "Are you sure? I can't— I mean, there's a whole outfit in here." She dug further into the bag. "There's *shoes*. Jasper, I can't accept this!"

Jasper had been ready for this. He braced himself against his dragon's crushing disappointment. It took a lot of human self-control not to take to the skies and go sulk on the highest mountain-top in the ranges, but he managed it.

He'd gone back to the store where he bought the gloves and scarf. He'd only meant to buy the matching hat for the scarf-and-gloves set. And then he'd remembered her stockinged legs, and wondered how windproof her navy-blue coat was…

He opened his mouth, a dozen pre-prepared arguments on the tip of his tongue. But before he could start, Abigail wrapped her arms around him, squeezing until he couldn't breathe.

"Thank you," she muttered into his chest. "This is *way* too much, and I don't know why you're bothering… but thank you." She pulled away and wiped her eyes quickly.

"I thought for a moment you were going to tell me to turn the car around and return them," Jasper joked. Were her eyes a little red? His dragon clacked its claws together nervously. Had his practical, definitely-not-a-Christmas-gift not been the right thing to do?

Abigail giggled. "I already saw that you're taken the tags off everything."

"And I paid in cash. *And* I lost the receipts. All of them." Abigail's giggle turned into a snort of laughter and the knot in Jasper's chest loosened. It was all right. "Come on. They should be ready for us by now."

He pushed through the door. The room inside was comfortably warm, blissful after the bite of cold outside. Flames crackled in a six-foot-wide fireplace, sending flickering light over a couple of temptingly deep armchairs and a thick patterned rug.

It would have been the perfect location for a quiet, private dinner; but that wasn't what Jasper had planned. He caught Abigail's eye and nodded towards the back window. She walked over, shopping bag clutched tightly to her chest.

The Puppy Express usually only ran during the day, but Jasper had made a few calls, and they'd agreed to stay open for one last, late-night ride. Abigail actually squealed with delight when she saw the team of huskies harnessed to the sled outside.

The manager strode up, a welcoming smile on his face. "Heartwell, party of two?"

Abigail slid her hand into Jasper's pocket and squeezed his hand. Warmth glowed inside him.

Jasper nodded to the manager. "Thanks for staying open this late. Is there somewhere my date—" Abigail squeezed his hand tighter, and the glow inside him burned brighter than the blazing fireplace. "— can get changed?"

"Right this way."

Jasper was tempted to follow Abigail into the changing room, but she fended him off, reminding him that they only had a few hours. So he chatted to the manager and accompanied him outside to pack the sled while his mate dressed herself in the clothes he had bought for her. His third gift to her. And the third gift she had accepted.

A blast of warm air hit his back as the door behind him swung open. He turned to see Abigail outlined by the glow of firelight.

He had been very careful. No Christmas colors, which was a difficult ask in a town like this. Soft pale cream for the warm, windproof jacket with a fur-lined hood, matching pants, a dove-grey hat to match her other accessories, and dark boots lined with thick, warm wool.

She looked magnificent.

Jasper took two long strides, and wrapped his hands around her waist. "Everything fits?"

"Perfectly." Her cheeks were pink as she pulled up the hood. "I'm impressed. Even I can't pick out clothes to fit me, half the time."

"All those hours exploring your body weren't a waste," he murmured into her ear, and her cheeks flared from pink to bright, pleased red. She poked him in the chest and he caught her finger to kiss it.

"Hey, lovebirds!" The Puppy Express manager whistled and eight pairs of eyes snapped to him: two humans', and six dogs'. Jasper laughed and linked his arm with Abigail's.

"Ready to go on an adventure?"

9

ABIGAIL

To Abigail's surprise, the manager handed the reins to Jasper.

"You're going to drive?"

Jasper raised both eyebrows at her. "Don't sound so shocked. I have done it before." His eyebrows knitted together. "Seven… eight years ago?"

"Mountains haven't changed since then," the manager said cheerily, slapping Jasper on the shoulder. "Lake's still in the same place. Caves not moved too much. Couple of trees have fallen down, but there's always more growing up to take their place."

Abigail looked from one man to the other. "Have you been here before?"

"I grew up around here." He moved closer and Abigail breathed him in, sweet and spice over the sharp bite of ice and snow. His mouth quirked. "Maybe if I'd stayed longer, instead of flying off to see the world, this wouldn't be only our third date."

Something like fire gleamed in his eye. Abigail glanced over her shoulder. Surely they weren't close enough to the window for the firelight to be reflecting in his eyes?

She turned back, and Jasper was holding out his hand to her, the other stretched out toward the sled. "My lady?"

Heat unspooled inside her as she took his hand, and he swept her into the sled's cushioned seat. The night was cold, but her new clothes were warmer than any winter gear she'd ever worn. Or maybe it wasn't the clothes. Maybe she was just so drunk with happiness that the cold didn't stand a chance.

Jasper jumped in beside her. She shouldn't have been able to feel the heat of his body through all the layers they were both wearing, but she thought she could. His knee pressed against hers and she laughed, pure joy bubbling out of her like champagne bubbles.

"It must be eleven by now, at least," she said, hiccupping back giggles. "And you're going to take me on a sleigh— sled ride, in the middle of the mountains, in the middle of the night? Should we file the missing person's report now, to save time in the morning?"

"You wound me," Jasper declared dryly. He let his head hang back with a sigh. "Very well. I admit it. We're doing the children's route— but *not* because my sixteen-year-old self's incredible dogsledding skills might be in any way less than magnificent."

He pecked her on the nose. "Because it's a half-hour loop, and I need to get you home before you turn into a pumpkin." He flicked the reins. "Hup!"

The dogs stayed where they were.

Abigail bit the inside of her cheek. Jasper glanced sideways at her, his cheeks going pink. "Er… mush?"

A whistle cut through the air, and all the huskies' ears pricked up. The manager was leaning back against the lodge wall, hands in his pockets. He grinned at Abigail and Jasper, whistled again, and the dogs leapt into action.

Jasper wound his arm around Abigail's shoulders, groaning. "Do me a favor and pretend that didn't happen," he muttered.

"Forget this?" She spread her arms. "Never. I'm going to remember every moment of it."

The night was dark. Snow-covered trees rising like shadowy giants either side of them, reaching for a star-filled sky. But they weren't driving into darkness. A lantern at the front of the sled lit the track directly in front of them, and hundreds of lights dangled from the lower branches of the trees, lighting their way through the forest. More lights glowed through the pines, hinting at twists and turns ahead.

The dogs were taking the trail at a placid trot, as though they'd done it a thousand times— Which they probably have, Abigail thought. How long do huskies live? Could these dogs, or their parents, have pulled Jasper around when he came here as a child?

The thought made her feel strange. Like her insides were shivering, half warm, half frozen. The idea of Jasper growing up here, in a town obsessed with Christmas— it felt so right. She'd seen how his eyes shone when he looked at the stupid decorations in the shops, and her ridiculous work uniform, even when she'd been scowling at them. He'd paraded around in that awful sweater like it was the Emperor's New Clothes.

And yet he'd gone such incredible lengths to keep their dates Christmas-free once he saw how much the holiday bothered her.

He was so full of warmth and kindness. A real, genuine good person.

Too good for you. Her stomach twisted.

Beside her, Jasper huffed. "I'd like to pretend that I'm steering, but… I think the dogs are on autopilot." He sighed and dropped the reins in his lap. "Well. This is less impressive than I intended."

"Is it like you remember?"

His eyes softened as he hugged her closer. "Better. And the less attention I have to keep on the track, the more attention I can give you…"

He tipped her head back and kissed her, and the cold shivery feeling in her stomach melted away.

The huskies knew the route like the back of their paws. Twenty minutes later, they pulled to the side of the track and came to a stop beside a frozen lake that looked like something…

Like something off of a Christmas card, Abigail thought, and a knot formed in her chest. She took a deep breath, rolling her shoulders back to relax herself. Her breath billowed out in front of her.

She would *not* ruin this. Not like last night, with the ice-skating carolers.

The air was crisp, without a trace of a breeze. The scene looked like someone had hit pause on the world: snow clung to black pine branches, ice stretched out over the lake. Abigail felt like she, Jasper and the dogs might be the only living things there; it was like they had stepped into another world, silent and serene and coldly beautiful.

The only movement was the heaving of the huskies' sides as they sat down in the snow, their breath forming clouds of vapor over their heads… and Jasper and her. Her lips were still tingling from his kisses.

He slipped his hand into hers. "Come on," he said. "I think our escort is suggesting we get out and stretch our legs."

Icy snow crunched under her boots as she stepped off the sled. The smell of pine filled her nose and she closed her eyes, drinking the world in through her other senses. She could almost taste the cold, all snow and ice and sharp pine, and—

A spicy sweetness that made her legs go weak. She leaned backwards, knowing Jasper was right behind her. His arms snuck around her, his lips nuzzling past her hood to brush against her neck. God, she loved how he couldn't keep his hands off her.

Maybe she'd been wrong, all these years, with her Christmas System. Falling into bed with someone was far more fun than working herself to exhaustion and hiding away…

No. Her stomach turned. Falling into bed with *Jasper*, that was one thing. But the thought of doing this with anyone else just felt wrong.

"What do you think?" Jasper murmured, nipping at her ear.

"What do I think?" She looked around. There was a small picnic area by the edge of the lake, a few low log seats around a blackened fire pit. Lights glittered on the trees like stars come down to rest. "I think it's beautiful. And that you probably brought every girl in town here, back when you were a sixteen-year-old dogsledder extraordinaire."

"Never!" Jasper spun her around. "You're the first woman I've ever brought here," he insisted, honesty radiating from his every pore.

Abigail stared hard at him. He stared back, all wounded innocence.

"Huh," she said at last, the corners of her mouth twitching. "Would that be because this is the kids' circuit, and usually it's chock-a-block with adorable, screaming children?"

"Ah, you got me." He groaned and leaned forward until his forehead tapped against hers. "Foiled again."

Abigail giggled, and then breathed in deep, inhaling his enticing, spicy scent and trying not to think too hard about the idea of Jasper taking other women on dates like this. Everything they'd done was so *new* for her, so spontaneous and joyful. She knew it was stupid to feel jealous over the idea of anyone else having these experiences with Jasper… but she couldn't help it. The only option was to ignore it.

"I wasn't lying, though." His fingers wounds around hers, and his breath whispered in her ear. "You're the first woman I've ever taken out here, kids' circuit or anywhere else. I wanted to do something special, just for you. Just for *us*." He kissed her and then darted away, graceful as a cat. He called back over his shoulder: "And that includes dinner!"

Abigail stared after him, head spinning. He— something special? This is something special?

It had always been special for her, of course: an unexpected, wonderful spark of light in the middle of the most miserable time of the year. But Jasper was, well, *Jasper*. He was good-looking, a charmer, and— her hands clenched inside her new designer gloves— obviously wealthy. He could have any woman he wanted, surely.

But he'd gone for her. *Something special, just for us.*

She felt like she was standing on the edge of a precipice. A fun fling, that was one thing. But something *special*? That was dangerous. Could she risk letting herself fall?

Especially at this time of year?

Jasper was untying something from the back of the sled. Abigail watched him, waiting for— For what? For a host of angels to descend from the sky, slap you upside the head, and tell you what to do with your life?

You've never had a single relationship that you haven't screwed up, one way or another. There's no way this one is going to go any better. Maybe I should just… enjoy it while I can.

Jasper glanced up at her and she looked away quickly, her cheeks burning. If he knew she'd been ogling him—

Then what? What's the worst that could happen? Not in a few days' time, not weeks or months from now. What's the worst that could happen, right now, from the hot guy who clearly likes you back knowing you enjoy looking at him?

Abigail took a deep breath and looked back at Jasper. His eyes were still on her, and when he met her gaze, fire seemed to kindle in their warm brown depths. His mouth opened slightly and the memory of his kisses was so strong Abigail could almost feel them on her lips. She lifted one gloved hand and touched her mouth, gently.

You're worried about falling? It's too late for that. You've already careened straight off that cliff.

Her gaze shifted sideways, past Jasper. She didn't want him to see the trepidation in her eyes.

Something behind him caught her attention. A distraction. *Thank God.*

"What's that?"

Jasper frowned slightly, and then followed her pointing finger to the small post-box nestled under a tree at the side of the track. The dogs had stopped the sled right beside it, and the only reason Abigail hadn't seen it before was because she'd gotten out on the lake side, and been distracted by the view.

"There can't seriously be postal service out— *oh.*" Abigail hit herself on the forehead as realization dawned. "I get it. Puppy Express. Like the Pony Express?" She walked over to the mailbox. There was a smaller wooden crate to one side, its waterproof lid weighted down with a large stone.

"Exactly right. But— and this is the most important part of the business model, I'm given to understand— literally ten thousand times cuter. I'm informed they measured that scientifically." Jasper came up and put his arm around her waist. He nodded at the smaller crate. "Postcards come free with the ride, and the manager will have them sent anywhere in town within a few days. I think he makes his staff drop them off on the way to work in the mornings. Which is a bit trickier for the ones addressed to the North Pole."

Abigail glanced sideways at Jasper. His eyes were lit up— the same way they did whenever he saw, talked about, or probably even *thought* about Christmas things. Hell, he probably had that hideous sweater with the dancing trees on under his gorgeous woolen jacket.

Abigail rocked back and forwards, her feet crunching in the snow. Then, before she could change her mind, she stepped forward and grabbed the rock off the crate, flipping back the lid. The box was piled high with stacks of postcards, carefully wrapped in waterproof plastic.

"Do you have a pen?" she asked Jasper, looking back at him over her shoulder. "And— what's your address in Pine Valley?"

His eyebrows knitted together. "You want to— ? But they're *Christmas* cards, I thought…"

"I want to write you one." Abigail held her breath. You're already falling. The landing is going to be hell. But that doesn't mean you can't enjoy the ride.

Jasper's whole face lit up, and Abigail knew she'd made the right decision. "There should be pens in there," he said. "Pass me one?"

Jasper took his postcard and pen and stood on the other side of the post box, using its sloped roof as a writing surface. Abigail stayed kneeling down by the postcard crate. She angled her body so that Jasper couldn't see what she was writing.

But what was she going to write?

Now that she had the pen in her hand, all inspiration fled. She didn't want to write some sappy, stereotypical message. Not the sort of thing you could find pre-printed in millions of cards around the world already. The look in Jasper's eyes when she said she wanted to write him a Christmas card— that deserved something special.

She closed her eyes, remembering their ice-skating date the night before. Coasting across the ice with her eyes closed— it had felt like flying. Like she could spread her arms and soar out over the snowy mountains, and leave the Christmas-infested town behind.

Don't mess this up, she told herself sternly, and began to draw.

She pushed the postcard through the slot face-down. Jasper pouted. "I don't get to see it?"

"Not until it's sent," she said, prickling. "Otherwise what's the point?" And besides, I don't want to see your face when you see it. Just in case I've just done the stupidest thing ever.

"Well, in that case…" Jasper clamped his postcard between his gloved hands and fed it through the slot, hiding his message from Abigail's view. "You'll just have to wait, too."

Abigail snorted. "I'm pretty sure that's how mail generally works, yeah."

Jasper turned to her. His eyes were brighter than she'd ever seen them. Almost— amber? But, no, amber wasn't the right word for that strange combination of chocolate brown, gold and orange-red.

"Thank you," he said softly. "I know you don't like Christmassy things and— well, I guess you figured out I'm kind of crazy about it…"

"Hey," she said, reaching out to cover his lips with her gloved fingers before the conversation could get any more awkward. "I'm not a total Grinch. I can allow myself *one* stupid Christmassy thing each year."

"Just the one?" Jasper's eyes sparkled as he nipped at her fingertips.

"Don't push it!" Abigail relaxed as Jasper laughed. So she'd written him a Christmas card. So what? It was just a card. It didn't mean anything. "Now, how about that dinner you promised me?"

Jasper leapt back to the sled and picked up the hamper he had been unpacking before she noticed the post box. As she watched, he hefted it in one arm and gestured with the other to the picnic site. "Shall we?"

Abigail rubbed her hands together and nodded. Her breath was forming such a thick fog in the crisp air, so she wasn't sure if he saw. But there were so many emotions fighting inside her, she didn't trust herself to speak.

Jasper grabbed a picnic blanket from the sled and arranged it on one of the log seats for her. While she sat down, he started unpacking the meal. The hamper steamed as he opened it, releasing mouth-watering smells.

"It's nothing fancy, I'm afraid. Beef stew. Sourdough. The wine *was* mulled, so I hope this thermos has done its thing. Though, if it hasn't, I guess cold mulled wine isn't too different from sangria…"

Abigail took a deep breath. "It all looks amazing," she said softly. Her voice didn't tremble at all. Encouraged, she went on, "And it *smells* amazing. God, I didn't realize how hungry I was."

He handed her a steaming thermos mug. "Then eat up."

The mulled wine was sweet and spicy and, yes, still hot. Abigail licked her lips, savoring the flavor. She opened her eyes to see Jasper's gaze locked on her mouth. His pupils were so huge they almost swallowed up the red-brown of his irises.

Abigail swallowed. *Something special.* Part of her was already clenched in fear, waiting for everything to go wrong. This was so clearly a bad idea. But part of her…

She licked her lips again, and a muscle in Jasper's jaw twitched. Excitement shot through her like lightning. Part of her really, *really* wanted to see where this went, before everything inevitably fell to pieces.

"Hey," she said, kicking him gently. "None of that. This is the *kids'* circuit, remember. Behave."

Jasper smiled wickedly. "It's also close to midnight, and the sky is full of stars. And it's very, very cold." He shuffled closer to her on the log until they were pressed together, his arm around her shoulder, his hip nudging up against hers. Abigail let her head fall onto his shoulder. "That's better."

"Mmm." Abigail closed her eyes. Jasper was reassuringly solid, warm and strong and… her heart trembled. *Special.* She knew she should explain to him why she had been acting like such an ass, but even the thought of it made her whole body suddenly heavy. Like she'd just run a marathon, not scribbled on a postcard.

The rich smell of beef stew rose up around her and she opened them again to see a spoon hovering in front of her face. "Hey!"

Jasper tutted. "You've been on your feet all day. From what you said about your boss, I bet you haven't had the chance to grab more than a few bites to eat since the start of your shift. I don't want you collapsing on me." He paused and Abigail got ready to groan, anticipating his next words. "…Not yet, anyway."

Abigail groaned. "I have work at nine again tomorrow."

"Then I intend to make the most of the time we have." He waved the spoon enticingly. "And you'll need your strength—"

Abigail rolled her eyes and grabbed the spoon. "You're such a romantic."

He snuck one hand up under her coat. "I try."

The meal was delicious— but it wasn't the hearty stew and bread that filled Abigail with a warm glow. It was long, slow looks Jasper sent her way, his eyes lingering on her lips. Every "accidental" brush of his hand against hers as they ate.

She could explain later. There wasn't any rush. And right now, with Jasper warm at her side, and

desire pooling hot inside her as they ate together…
she didn't want to ruin this.

Later, she promised herself.

Despite the food and Jasper's tempting small caresses, Abigail was almost dozing by the time they finished the meal. She leaned heavily on him as they walked back up to the sled, and once they were there it was all she could do not to curl up on the seat and fall asleep.

"Abigail?"

"Hmm?" She rubbed her eyes and blinked hard. Jasper settled his arm over her shoulder. She thought he was moving a bit more slowly than earlier. Tentative.

Or maybe he's just as full and sleepy as I am.

"What is it?" she asked, wriggling into his side. She loved the sound of his voice: so smooth and rich. Like chocolate. Warm, melting chocolate…

"I wanted to ask you about…" Jasper's voice trailed off. His chest rose and fell. "Have you enjoyed tonight?"

"God, yes. It's been… perfect." Abigail snuggled closer into him. "I wish it didn't have to end."

"Do you think—" Jasper tapped his teeth together, breaking off again. He sighed. "I can't believe you've been here all along. All those years, if I'd just come *home*, I could have found you here."

"Falling off a roof," Abigail murmured, and chuckled. Jasper nudged her.

"Well I didn't know you made a habit of *that*. Who's been catching you, previous years?"

This time, Abigail didn't catch the yawn before it escaped. She fleetingly wondered whether to tell Jasper about the other pain-in-the-ass things Mr. Bell had made her do during the holiday season, but decided against it. *No need to ruin the moment by being a killjoy.*

"This is the first year we did the whole rooftop display thing," she said instead. "I've only fallen off step-ladders before. I levelled up this year."

"Lucky me."

She giggled. "Lucky *me*, that you were there." She yawned again. *Eyes open,* she told herself. *Come on. Look around you. How can you miss all of this, just for a bit of sleep? A bit of…* She shook her head. "Wait, what was it you wanted to ask me? Did I miss the question?"

Jasper's warm chocolate tones washed over her. If she turned her head, she thought, maybe she could press her face up against his neck, and feel his voice reverberating against her skin…

The unmistakable tune of *Jingle Bell Rock* woke her up. For a moment, she had no idea where she was. Then she realized how warm her bum was.

"When did we get back in the car?" she mumbled sleepily. "And when— we're back in town?" She blinked, peering out the windows. They were less than a block from her apartment. Her chest went tight. *How could I fall asleep? God, he probably thinks I'm such a—*

"Sorry about that." Jasper's hand reached into her field of vision and he turned off the radio. "Sleep well?"

"I—" Abigail stifled a yawn. "Did you carry me off of the sled?"

"I was sure you'd wake up, but you were out like a light." Jasper engaged the handbrake and leaned over to kiss her. "Sleeping beauty."

Abigail snorted. "Now I know you're lying."

"Peaceful. Elegant. Only very minimal amounts of drool."

"Oh, God." Abigail covered her face with her hands— and swiped surreptitiously at her mouth. Her glove came away dry. No drool. Thank goodness. "I can't believe I fell asleep in the middle of our date. You put so much effort into organizing everything— the food, the dogsledding— and I just straight-up passed out. I'm a lousy date."

"Don't be sorry. If you needed to sleep, you needed to sleep." He grinned and touched her cheek. The gold and red sparks were gone from his eyes, but— Abigail blinked. She must have been completely wrong when she thought his eyes were brown. They were the color of a low fire, just beginning to flicker out. No gold and red sparks, just a soft, inviting glow that warmed her from the inside out.

She frowned, remembering. "Did you have something you wanted to ask me?"

Jasper's eyes widened. He opened his mouth— and then shut it again. "It can wait," he murmured. "The important thing is, I got you back home before you turned into a pumpkin."

Abigail looked out the window. There was her apartment: plain white walls, dark unlit windows. She still had to put her uniform in the laundry, and…

A vision of a small mountain cottage formed in her mind. Jasper's bachelor pad— the one he must have hardly spent any time at since he arrived in Pine Valley. She made up details, matching them to the man sitting beside her in the car.

Solid wooden walls, and thick, luxurious rugs on the floor. A roaring fire, for sure. Deeply cushioned chairs, and a kitchen stocked with everything you would need for a holiday cut off from the world by snow.

And Christmas decorations. She bet that even if he hadn't had time for anything else, he had a tree. She closed her eyes, imagining. Would there be stockings over the fireplace? No, he was here visiting family, wasn't he? The stockings would be in their house.

Well, that was the sensible option, at least. Was it the option that a man who'd bought her expensive gifts on a few days' acquaintance would take? Or would he fill every inch of his life with Christmas cheer and generosity, regardless of double-ups?

Her heart ached. It wasn't worth even wishing he'd taken her there, instead of here to her cold, empty apartment. She wouldn't fit in anywhere like that.

She opened her eyes. Jasper's ember-like gaze burned into her. Maybe she didn't fit into his world—but he could fit into hers. At least until he figured out how badly they were matched.

"Do you want to come up?" she asked, her voice rough.

Jasper smiled. "Always."

IO

JASPER

DECEMBER 23

TWO DAYS UNTIL CHRISTMAS

Jasper couldn't stop looking at his phone. He'd wheedled Abigail's phone number out of her that morning, after buttering her up with a pile of freshly made breakfast biscuits and creamy hot coffee. Not that she had required much wheedling. The moment he pulled his phone out, her cheeks had gone pink, and by the time she finished putting her number in, even the tip of her adorable upturned nose was blushing.

But that wasn't the best thing. No, the best thing was the message she had sent him mid-afternoon.

Can I organize the date tonight? I have an idea I think you'll like.

Excitement fizzed over his skin. Nothing he put together could be as wonderful as this. His mate was letting down her prickly façade. Reaching out to him.

He couldn't wait to see what she had planned.

"Uncle Ja-a-a-asper!" The warning came just in time. Jasper leapt back, shoving his phone safely into a pocket as a thick slurry of snow slid off the roof of the lodge.

Well, partly snow. Mostly, it was Cole. The little dragon tumbled tail-over-snout, covered in wet slush.

"Cole! Watch out!"

Jasper braced himself. His dragon rose up inside him, so close to the surface that scales shimmered on his skin. He forced it back down. His mate had given him her phone number. That was a *gift*, and that gift was on his phone. And his phone would be safe in his pocket, *unless* he shifted, in which case his clothing would be ripped to shreds and his phone would be left to the mercy of the elements. The elements and a juvenile dragon shifter.

Besides, his human form was sturdy enough to deal with one four-year-old dragon—

"Oof!"

Jasper flew backwards as Cole slammed into him. He hit the ground, a hundred pounds of dragon on his chest. Luckily, the snow was deep enough up here by the lodge to cushion his fall.

Jasper pushed himself up, fighting against the combined weight of his nephew and the drifts of snow. Cole's claws punctured his jacket as he tried to keep his balance. Jasper carefully put one hand over the pocket where he had stowed his phone.

"What's the matter, buddy? You forget how to use your wings?"

Cole shook snow off his snout. His dragon was as black as his namesake, gleaming with green and red undertones. His wings flexed, sending more wet snow into the air.

I was hiding! he announced triumphantly, his eyes glittering blue-black. *And I gotted you, uncle Jasper!*

"Hiding so well you got your wings snow-logged and couldn't get them out in time, huh?" Jasper winced. When he'd decided to stay human, he had kind of relied on his nephew *flying* into him, not falling with all of his considerable draconic weight. *Ouch.*

Cole leapt off Jasper and pranced through the snow. *I gotted you! I gotted you!*

"Oh, you did, huh?" Jasper rolled onto his feet. His chest ached a bit— but it was only a bruise. He scooped up an armful of snow. "Let's see how you like a taste of your own medicine— hah!"

He launched the giant snowball directly at Cole's face. The snowball exploded on impact, covering the small dragon from snout to hindquarters. The only part of him left visible were his wings, flapping in surprise either side of the heap of snow. *Uncle Ja-a-a-asper! That's not fair! I wasn't ready!*

Cole wriggled butt-first out of the snow, his tail whipping back and forth. He shook himself, but a crust of snow stuck above his eye-ridges, making him look like he had giant woolly eyebrows. *Okay, now I'm going to go back on the roof and you walk around again and I'll jump on you!*

Without waiting for an answer, Cole bounded off. Jasper laughed and dusted himself off.

"Hey, Jasper!"

"Hank!" Jasper waved to his brother-in-law, who was pushing a wheelbarrow full of firewood up to the lodge.

Hank set the wheelbarrow down a few feet away. His eyes flicked from Jasper, who was still mostly covered in snow, up to the lodge roof. "You and Cole having fun?"

Hank was a dragon shifter. He had been part of the family for six years, ever since Opal dragged him back to the lodge after one spring break with the news that she had found her mate, and they were getting married *right now,* so everyone hurry up and put on some nice clothes, and also she was taking him up to her hoard straight after so no one had better interrupt them. Jasper had never seen his sister happier, or more gleefully officious.

His brother-in-law was a massive man, broad-shouldered and with a red-brown beard that made him look more like a lumberjack than a dragon. His dragon had pine-green scales and eyes the color of new spring growth. The *classic model of dragon*, Opal called him.

"Fun's one word for it," Jasper said ruefully, brushing snow off his shoulders. "He's enjoying himself."

Hank nodded at the wheelbarrow. "Thought you might want some fuel for the cottage. Though from what Opal says, you haven't been using it much." He grinned. "Busy in town, huh? You planning on dragging her over to meet the family soon?"

"Soon." Jasper's stomach clenched. "I just have to…"

He sagged, remembering the night before. He had meant to tell her then. Tell her *everything*. The Puppy Express was far enough out of town that he wouldn't have risked anyone seeing him shift— except the manager, and he was an old family friend.

But then Abigail had written him a Christmas card. He hadn't even received it yet, but Jasper already knew it would be the most precious thing he had ever owned. A Christmas card, from his mate who hated Christmas.

She was just starting to let down her walls. Maybe even trust him. And after she had fallen asleep in his arms, in the dogsled… he hadn't wanted to ruin that moment by telling her about the curse.

Hank caught his eye and nodded. "I figured as much." He let out a huff of breath and hooked his thumbs into his pockets. "You want to talk about it?"

Jasper sighed. "Not where we might get dive-bombed by a mad dragon any moment."

"Fair enough." Hank clapped him on the shoulder. "Let's go work on the bonfire."

Ten minutes later, they were out of range of Cole's snow-monster attacks, but Jasper was no closer to putting words to the conflict raging inside him. Hank dumped an armful of branches in front of the half-built bonfire and crouched down to sort through them.

"I'm going to tell her," Jasper said at last. He aimed a kick at a snowdrift. "Tonight." He hesitated again. "Some of it, at least."

He glanced back at Hank. His brother-in-law looked completely engrossed in his task.

"No, I have to tell her all of it. And if I tell her tonight, that still leaves all of Christmas Eve for us to… plan things," he went on, shoving his hands in his pockets and stamping down the snow around the bonfire. "That's still in time. Just. No, it'll be fine. I'll tell her—"

He found himself aiming a kick at the carefully arranged pile of wood, and quickly changed direction.

"I'll tell her I'm a shifter, at least. I can't hide that."

Hank grunted. "And?"

"And…" Jasper swore. "And what? Isn't that likely to blow her mind enough?"

Hank rested his elbows on his knees and looked up at him. "Jas, you've had three days with her. From memory, those first few days are the craziest of your life. Your dragon's going mad, your human isn't much better— and you've got the deadline on top of that. So tell me how you've managed not to tell her *any* of it yet."

Jasper blinked. He wasn't sure he'd ever heard Hank string so many words together at once.

And he didn't know what to say back.

"I—" He stopped and swallowed hard. "You and Opal had it easy. She didn't have to turn your world upside down. You already knew about shifters, you already knew about mates… you saw each other, and bam, the curse was broken."

"Your sister never told me about the curse."

"What?" Jasper stared, too shocked to close his mouth. "You're kidding. Opal?"

Hank looked up at him, his green eyes sober. "She was scared, Jas. The mate bond was one thing, but she thought if I knew about the curse…" He sighed.

"Honestly? I don't know. She *still* won't explain what she was thinking. But I'd bet half my hoard that she was scared I'd run off, if I knew that I was all that stood between her and a life as half a person."

"Hell."

"Yep."

Jasper crouched down next to his brother-in-law. "So when did you find out?"

"That's not the point of the story, Jas. We're talking about you." Hank sighed. "Opal nearly had a heart attack when she saw you'd come home alone. I could feel her all the way from the lodge. She thought she was going to lose you. Calmed down a bit when you found your girl, but you're running out of time."

Jasper's heart twisted. He hadn't even noticed that Opal was still upset; he thought she'd put aside her fears when he found Abigail.

Hank snorted. "And don't go saying you didn't even notice she was stressed over it. You know she keeps things close to the chest."

"I'll tell her. Christmas Eve. It's all going to be fine," he said quickly, standing up and pushing his hands into his pockets.

"Why not tonight? Bring her over for brunch tomorrow. It'll make your sister *feel* better." Hank stood up and started weaving branches into the bonfire. "Don't leave it to the last minute, Jas. Trust me on this."

Jasper sat on one of the low benches under the massive plastic Christmas tree, staring across at Abigail's shop. He could see her inside, bustling around helping the last customers of the day. The smile on her face looked strange, and it had taken him a while to recognize why. It wasn't the same smile that lit up her face when she saw him. It wasn't *real*. The edges of her mouth might be pulled up, but her eyes were tired. *Her Christmas smile?* Jasper thought sadly, remembering everything she had said about the holiday being fake.

Double shifts in the week before Christmas? he thought, cradling his Rudolph Special. That's crazy. Even I think that's crazy. No wonder she was asleep on her feet last night.

He checked his watch. Five minutes to the end of her shift. He'd already seen Mr. Bell leave; Abigail was alone in the shop. He'd bought a coffee for her, too, and didn't want it to get cold.

His dragon itched to go to her, but he knew she wouldn't thank him for distracting her as she tried to get rid of her final customers.

At last the final lingering shoppers drifted out the doors, and the main lights in the shop turned off. Jasper could still see Abigail's shape, silhouetted by the lights of the shop's Christmas tree, as she made her final rounds. She locked the door, pulled down the security grill, and went to tap a few final times at the checkout computer.

Then she looked up.

Jasper was twenty, maybe thirty feet away. Abigail was backlit by the blinking tree lights; he couldn't see her face. But he knew that she had seen him, because his dragon was suddenly hammering at his chest to be let out.

Not now! Jasper pushed it back, but his skin was fizzing, like he was close to a shift. He flexed his hands, concentrating on them staying hands, and not stretching out into scaled claws.

Abigail raised one hand and waved at him. Jasper barely got himself under control before she disappeared into the back of the shop.

"Jasper!" Abigail appeared around the side of the shop, beckoning him over. Jasper loped across the square and pulled her into his arms, careful to keep the two takeaway coffee cups upright. She was wearing the coat he had bought her, but hadn't stopped to do it up, and he could see her work uniform underneath it.

Abigail kissed him and then pulled back, her cheeks pink. "I thought I'd never get rid of those last two customers. I hope you weren't waiting long."

"Forever. I'm frozen stiff." He nuzzled her ear. "Only the thought of you warming me up kept me from giving up and turning into a snowman. Also, this ridiculous drink."

He held the two drinks up in front of her. Abigail's eyebrow rose. "What are these?"

"Coffees."

"Are you sure?" She pulled the lid off the one he offered her. "Coffee and… red stuff?"

"Try it."

She shot him a doubting look, but took a sip. Jasper waited as she licked cream off her lips. "That is definitely not coffee," she announced. "But… it's not bad. Is that a glace cherry?"

"It's a Rudolph Surprise," Jasper explained. Abigail looked pained. "…That's his nose."

Abigail rolled her eyes. She reached in and plucked the cherry from the drink, and then bit her lip, her eyes flicking to meet Jasper's. "Do you want it?"

She lifted the cherry to Jasper's lips. Sugar burst onto his tongue, the sickly sweet, unmistakable red flavor of glace cherry. Jasper's mouth filled with saliva and he gulped.

"I'll drink the rest of it, though," Abigail said with a teasing smile. "Thank you."

Jasper licked his lips and coughed. "Since you're putting on tonight's entertainment, I figured the least I could do was bring coffee."

"I'm not going to fall asleep on you this time, I promise." Abigail took another sip of the frothy, creamy drink, and grimaced. "Not that I think this has been anywhere near a coffee bean. But the sugar will help."

"So long as you stay awake long enough to let me know where we're driving." Jasper pulled Abigail's coat closed. The hints of her body under the skimpy elf costume were enticing, but he didn't want her to get cold. Time to get going. I can't wait to see what my mate has planned…

Abigail's voice broke through his thoughts. "We're not going anywhere."

Jasper frowned. Abigail was smiling— and she'd already shut up the shop, so it couldn't be that she had to work extra late tonight. But there was a wobbly edge to her smile, like whatever scheme she had cooked up, she was starting to regret it.

He couldn't let that happen.

"What's the plan?" he said, tugging on the lapels of Abigail's coat until she leaned into him. She pressed her nose into his scarf.

"I want to show you something," she mumbled, her voice muffled by his scarf. "God, this seems like such a stupid idea now…"

"No idea of yours could be stupid," Jasper reassured her. She snorted and tipped her head back so he could see her roll her eyes.

"You just say that because you haven't heard it yet." Abigail bit her lip and squeezed her eyes shut. "Okay. Screw it. Follow me."

She kissed him again, and then grabbed his hand and pulled him down the alley. She stopped at the far end and fumbled a set of keys out of her pocket. "You're not allowed to tell anyone we did this," she warned him with a nervous grin. She lowered her voice as she turned the key in the lock. "The last thing I need is Mr. Bell turning my stupid idea into some sort of new attraction for the shop next year."

She yanked the door open and turned to Jasper. "Ready to peek behind the curtain?"

The shop's back rooms were cramped and small, nothing like the bright, glittering public-facing space. Broken-down cardboard boxes and pallets lined the walls nearest the alley entrance, and further in were replaced by tall piles of product boxes. The piles were so tightly crammed in that Jasper could hardly walk straight without bumping into something. After a tower of festive cookie jars almost came tumbling down on him, he crossed his arms tightly and started walking crab-wise down the passageways.

"You've still got this much stock, right before Christmas?"

Abigail ducked around a corner. Her voice filtered back through the stacks. "Christmas Eve is the busiest shopping day of the year up here. Everyone realizes they forgot to buy a Santa present for their least-favorite child, or an extra relative turns up out of the blue ready to ruin the day if they're not waited on hand and foot…"

Jasper carefully followed her around the corner and found her in the middle of grabbing her bag off a hook on the wall. She checked inside it for something, and then closed it quickly, flashing a nervous grin at him.

"Admiring our staff room? Look, we've got a seat and everything this year."

She moved aside to reveal a low wooden bench pushed up against the wall. It was already occupied: by a stack of Christmas card packs. Jasper blinked. Was this the only staff area in the shop? No wonder Abigail was so exhausted in the evenings.

His dragon's scales prickled inside him. This was unacceptable. Shops like this brought so many people joy— ever since he met Abigail, he'd noted how many people he saw around town carrying bags from the store she worked at. And all the employees got was a hard bench and a single coat hook between them?

He smiled and winked at Abigail before his unhappiness could creep onto his face. "There's not much room, but if I sit down first, you can always take my knee. It's bony, I warn you, but still probably better than that bench."

Abigail snorted and poked him in the side. "This isn't it. I was just grabbing my bag. Follow me upstairs."

She squeezed past him and back through the towering maze of boxes. A narrow staircase led up to an equally cramped second floor, but Abigail didn't pause at any of the doors leading off the landing. Instead she stopped in front of what looked like a blank wall.

"Even if you think this is stupid, you're not allowed to tell me, okay?" she said. It sounded like a joke, but her eyes were wary.

"This… wall?"

Abigail made a short, sharp noise of frustration. "No, the— I'm too short, I need you to pull it down." She pointed up at the ceiling.

"A trapdoor?" Jasper reached up and grabbed hold of the handle. "You could have said—"

"Look out!"

He was already pulling on the handle. Abigail slammed into him, pushing them both back down the corridor as a retractable ladder slid at top speed through the air where his head had been a second before.

"Oh my God." Abigail flung her arms around him, squeezing him so tight he could hardly breath. His shifter senses flared, and suddenly her heartbeat was so loud in his ears it might as well have been his own, thudding hard and fast with adrenaline. "That almost— this is such a bad idea, I'm sorry, we should just leave now—"

Jasper took her face in his hands. Her lips were thin with strain, and she wouldn't meet his eyes. "No," he said softly. "I want to see this through. Even if I have to risk decapitation by ladder." He stroked his thumb across her cheek. "Neither of us are having much luck with ladders this week, are we?"

"Nope." Abigail chuckled weakly. "God, we're not even meant to be up here in the first place— if I had to call Mr. Bell and tell him I'd murdered a potential customer in the shop after hours…" She flung her head back and groaned. "I would be so fired."

"Hmm. Tempting." Jasper tapped her lips and Abigail's head snapped back up. She raised her eyebrows.

"What?"

"Well, if I was haunting the shop, it would mean I didn't have to wait until ten in the evening to see you each day." He paused, putting on a serious, thinking face. "Of course, I would be dead in this scenario, so, not ideal…"

"Not ideal, no." Abigail bit her lip, and then gently pulled his hands away from her face. She took a deep breath that Jasper suspected was only partly a put-on. "Come on, then. Follow me."

She slung her back securely over her back and started up the ladder. Jasper stepped back, admiring the view— and then stepped smartly forward again.

The last time Abigail had gone up a ladder, she'd almost been badly injured. Enticing as the view was, it was more important that she feel safe. Jasper steadied the ladder with one hand, resting the other on Abigail's hip as it came level with his shoulders.

Abigail peered down at him and rolled her eyes— but her cheeks were pink. She was pleased. And so was Jasper. Forget watching her from a few steps away; the view from up close was a thousand times as good.

Abigail kept climbing— and Jasper kept his hand where it was. He caressed the generous curve of her ass, and her thick, beautiful thighs. The hem of her tunic hitched under his fingers, and then he was running his hand over the back of her knee, the round curve of her calf sloping down to her ankle…

Jasper bit back a groan. Her legs looked amazing in those candy-stripe stockings. But they felt even better, and now all he wanted was to tear them off her.

"Are you coming?" Abigail called down from the top of the ladder.

II

ABIGAIL

Abigail jiggled her feet as Jasper climbed up the ladder. This was such a stupid idea. God, it was the worst idea she'd ever had. Why was she doing this?

Jasper's head appeared through the trapdoor, and there was her answer. Because of *him*. Because he made her feel like no one else ever had before.

Because she was so close to having a happy Christmas, it hurt.

She watched Jasper carefully as he climbed up into the small attic room. This was about to go terribly wrong, she knew it. Her heart thudded in her throat.

Jasper's ember-like eyes moved around the room. The walls were peeling, cheap old paint flaking off in strips. There was no insulation— she'd left her jacket on for a reason, and now her and Jasper's breath mingled in white clouds.

No furniture. No carpet or wallpaper. Even the light coming in through the three small, round windows seemed muffled and flat.

Abigail bit her lip, wondering how long it would take Jasper to figure out where he was— and what his reaction would be.

"This is… nice," he said diplomatically. Abigail bit back a nervous smile as he stepped carefully around the trapdoor and did up her jacket. "It's…" She watched him hunt for something complimentary to say about the cold, bare attic. "Hang on. Where *are* we?"

"Above the shop." Abigail rocked back and forth on the balls of her feet.

"But there isn't anything above the shop. It's only two levels from the outside. The only thing above that is—" Jasper's eyes widened. Abigail's stomach fluttered as he darted to the nearest window. "Abigail, be honest with me… am I staring out at the square through Santa Claus's stomach?"

"Yes!" Abigail covered her mouth. The word had come out *far* too excited. Because *she* was far too excited, about this little, stupid thing. Sneaking up to the shop attic like a couple of teenagers. It was idiotic. So why was her head spinning?

Because you want this to work. Because you think it's going to work, and that's the stupidest thing of all.

She shook her head, trying to dislodge the nasty, vindictive voice, and bit her lip. When she looked up, Jasper was staring at her, an uncertain look in his eyes.

Jasper stuck his hands in his pockets and looked around the small attic slowly, his eyebrows furrowing. "This isn't…" He stopped and rubbed his forehead, staring appealingly at Abigail. Then he sighed and gestured around the tiny room. "Is this how you see Christmas? Festive and fun on the outside, barren and cold inside?"

Abigail's mouth fell open. She snapped it shut, wrapping her arms around her. "No," she burst out. "No, I just— I wanted to—" She paused and swallowed hard, willing the sudden queasiness in her stomach away. When she spoke again, her voice was small. "I thought you would like it. That you'd think it was… fun."

And see where that got you.

Jasper thought she'd planned this as some sort of jab at Christmas. At *him*. She couldn't even bear to look at him, remembering the stricken look on his face as he looked around the attic. As he looked at *her*.

What must he think of her? What kind of monster did he think she was?

Her shoulders slumped.

"Abigail—"

She didn't hear Jasper move, but suddenly his arms were around her, surrounding her with his warmth and strength. She took a deep, ragged breath, burying her face in his chest.

Jasper's hand landed tentatively on her head, stroking her hair softly. His heart beat against her cheek.

"I think it's wonderful," he said softly. "I think you're wonderful. Thank you for bringing me up here."

"You're thanking me for almost getting you decapitated, and then making you think I'm insulting you?"

Abigail squeezed her eyes shut. She kept them shut as Jasper slid one hand up to her chin and tipped her head back.

"My head is still where it's meant to be, but that didn't stop me being an idiot. Forgive me?" He kissed the tip of her nose, and then brushed his lips over her eyelids. Her nose twitched as his breath tickled it. "This is the sweetest, sexiest thing anyone has ever done for me," he whispered, and kissed her.

Abigail melted into the kiss. She didn't believe him— her idea was ridiculous and stupid and almost ended in disaster, not sweet or sexy. But if her stupid plan made him want to kiss her… well, she could live with that.

Jasper's lips were soft and every moment they were pressed against hers, her body seemed to become softer, too: the knots in her shoulders dissolved, the tension in her forehead melted away, and even the aches and pains in her feet from running after customers all day faded away.

She ran her hands up Jasper's chest, fingers pressing into his coat to feel the muscles beneath. A small moan of happiness escaped her lips.

Jasper's arms tightened around her. His tongue flicked out between her lips and Abigail's moan turned into a delighted gasp. She pressed against him, fingers tangling in his jacket, going up on tip-toes as their kiss became more passionate.

Jasper grabbed her around the waist and took advantage of her unstable position to tip her back, pushing her against the attic wall. Abigail nipped his lower lip, making him groan. They were pressed close enough together that she felt him go hard. She rolled her hips against him, excitement shivering inside her. How was it that this man she'd only met a few days ago could make her feel so good, at the worst time of the year?

She slid her hand up over his collarbone, worming her fingers in under his scarf to brush against his neck. Her fingertips scratched up against the stubble under his jaw and his pulse pounded against her touch, fast and urgent.

Jasper murmured something that she couldn't hear, but she felt the reverberation through her fingers.

"Hmm?" she asked wordlessly, and he groaned in response. He stepped forward, one hand pressing against the wall as he—

"Ugh!" Abigail flinched forward as icy water cascaded down the back of her neck. It dripped down her back, like frigid fingers clawing at her skin. Shuddering, Abigail tried to wipe the water away, twisting her spine to stop the icy fingers reaching further. She overbalanced and her foot slipped.

Jasper's arms were around her at once. He pulled her to him. Abigail hissed as he crushed her now-clammy tunic against her back.

"Ugh— What the hell? Where did that come from?"

Jasper let her go, but kept one hand on her waist. He held up the hand he had rested on the wall and shook it, sending droplets flying.

"The wall's soaking wet," he muttered. "Are you— look out!"

Abigail had turned around to look at the wall. As she moved her feet a floorboard groaned under her. Jasper swept her backwards, setting her down closer to the trapdoor.

Jasper knelt quickly and rapped on the floor. "We're over a strut here, I think— it should be sturdier."

"Thanks," Abigail gasped. She stared at the floorboards. They looked fine— but they had felt, just for a moment, like they were collapsing under her. What the hell was going on?

Abigail wiped the back of her neck, trying to swipe away as much of the water as she could. It felt like someone had dumped a bucket down her back. But where had that much water come from?

She fumbled her phone out of her bag, wiping her hands dry on her jacket before she turned on the flashlight app. The harsh LED illuminated what the light filtering in from the square hadn't shown.

The walls and ceiling of the attic space were glistening with water. What Abigail had thought was the stickiness of an unwashed floor was more water, soaking through the floorboards. "Hell," she muttered.

"It looks worst in that corner." Jasper pointed. He frowned, swearing under his breath. "I'd guess the roof's been damaged—"

"—But no one's noticed, because the Santa mannequin's covering it up. Heat rises through the shop, melts the snow on the roof display... and it drips straight through." Abigail bit the inside of her cheek. "Shit. Shit, shit, shit. How long has it been like this?"

Jasper knelt down and reached one hand out to the floor. He gave a particularly dark patch an experimental thud. It sounded like a rotten squash. "Long enough for this wood to be spongy."

"If we'd been standing half a foot farther left, we might have fallen through," Abigail whispered. Her stomach went tight and cold.

"Abigail—" Jasper stood up carefully and put his arm around her waist. "I think we should go down now."

He made her go down first. Abigail ran her hands along a few of the rungs as she hurried down. She'd thought the aluminum ladder was cold, when she was climbing it earlier— now she noticed the droplets of water. Not condensation. Melted snow.

She clenched her fists as she stepped off the ladder, and glanced up. Jasper was following her, but she couldn't wait for him. She had to check the other rooms.

"Shit."

By the time Jasper found her she was standing on the desk in Mr. Bell's office, testing the ceiling. Plaster came away in damp clumps at her touch. She met his eyes.

"It's not just the attic." Abigail groaned as she clambered down from the desk. "The display must be too heavy for the roof. Maybe the tiles have cracked, or someone hammered nails into something they shouldn't have, but... the whole ceiling's soaking. How the hell did no one *notice* this?"

Guilt twisted inside her faster than she could push it back. *You should have noticed something. You know Mr. Bell doesn't pay attention to regulations. You have to look after yourself. You, you, you—*

Abigail pressed the heels of her hands into her eyes, willing the voice to go away. "We should go outside," she muttered. "I don't feel safe here, knowing the roof's holding that much water."

She put her head down and hurried through the door, past Jasper. He put his hand on her lower back and kept pace with her as they descended the stairs to the ground floor. Abigail tried not to flinch. She knew he meant it as a comfort, but the discovery of the leaking roof had left her wound so tight she thought she might crack.

And it was Christmas Eve tomorrow. And if the roof was really bad, if Mr. Bell had to shut the shop...

She squeezed her eyes shut as she pushed through the external door into the alleyway. Cold air bit at her face. *If the shop's shut... what the hell am I meant to do tomorrow?*

Jasper turned her around to face him. She tried to get her face under control— God knew all her time in retail meant she could do that, at least— but he must have sensed her distress. Concern flooded his ember-warm eyes.

"It's not your fault, Abigail. You can't be blamed for not noticing it until now— none of your colleagues did either, right? And if you're worried about what your boss might say about you poking around after hours, hell, he must know it's a good thing we found the leak. Better now than when the shop's full of customers."

Abigail shook her head. "I'm not worried about that. I—" She wrapped her arms around herself as the cold night air bit into her, and began to gnaw on the inside of her cheek again. Now that she'd had a few minutes to think, she wasn't worried about Mr. Bell being angry at no one noticing the leak until now. The shop was so crazy this time of year, no one had time to breathe, let alone look up. And even if they had noticed any random drips, they probably would have assumed it was just customers tracking snowmelt into the store and flinging it around.

No. That wasn't the problem.

She groaned, biting down on her cheek. "It's Christmas Eve tomorrow. I'm meant to work all day. But this…"

"Hey." Jasper cupped her face in his hands. He tapped her cheek with his thumb until she stopped biting it. "So you might have a day off. Would it really be that bad?"

Yes. Abigail clenched her jaw shut before the word could get out.

Jasper was amazing, but tomorrow was Christmas Eve. He'd want to spend it with his family, not her.

And she couldn't wait around at home all day, with nothing to do. She *couldn't.*

She took a deep breath. Best case scenario, the shop was fine. They would open in the morning as usual. Double shift, no time off. Maybe she could even put in some extra hours cleaning up the upper floor.

Worst case scenario…

"I need to call my boss," she said stiffly, shoulders knotting. Jasper was holding her still, but his touch wasn't relaxing her like it did before. Instead, she could feel herself prickling. And every time she thought about tomorrow, it got worse.

Jasper's voice interrupted her crackling, unhappy thoughts. "Tell me what I can do."

He stared deep into her eyes. There wasn't any subterfuge in his gaze. He wasn't fidgeting to leave, or hiding impatience at their make-out session being interrupted by a flooded roof-space.

Which made what Abigail had to say even harder. "I need you to leave." She choked the words out.

Jasper moved his hands to her shoulders. For a moment, he didn't speak. Then he tightened his grip. A muscle in his jaw tensed. "I'm not going to leave you to deal with this by yourself."

"Well, too bad. You have to." An icy wind whistled down the alleyway. Abigail pulled away from Jasper, buttoning her jacket up higher around her neck. "This— this was a bad idea. All of it. And I can't deal with you being here right now, on top of everything else. Please."

Jasper reached out to her— and then closed his fist, and thrust both hands into his jacket pockets. Was it her imagination, or was he shaking?

He was cold. That must be it. They were both freezing out here, wet from the attic and chilled by the wind.

"You should go home," she said. The words came out harsher than she meant, and she winced. She should be growling at herself, not him. She didn't really want him to go. Or, since he had to, she wished he would go to her apartment, and be waiting for her when she got home.

She opened her mouth and her throat went dry. She couldn't say it. Not now, not with everything else that was happening.

"You want me to go." Jasper's voice was hollow.

Abigail couldn't speak. She nodded, her neck stiff and Jasper let out a sharp breath. For a moment, he looked as though he was about to say something else— then he shuddered and strode past her, stumbling slightly on the rubbish-strewn ground.

Abigail wished the ground would swallow her. She turned after Jasper as he marched away, like a flower turning hopelessly towards the sun. "Jasper, I—"

At the end of the alleyway, Jasper stumbled, steadied himself on the nearest wall— and didn't look back. In the space between one heartbeat and another, he was gone.

She watched the space where he had been, ice forming around her heart. Her vision swam.

He left.

Her breath caught and suddenly she couldn't hear anything but her pulse, pounding like a drum in her ears. She covered her face with her hands and forced herself to breath slowly.

She had to call Mr. Bell. That was the important thing, here. Call Mr. Bell, and hope like hell the shop would be open tomorrow.

That was the most important thing. Wasn't it?

12

JASPER

The curse shook him like a terrier with a rat. Jasper clutched at his dragon, trying desperately to hold onto it— but the shuddering power that took hold of him was too strong.

He was going to shift. Either that, or— *No!*

Scales crackled out of his skin. Jasper hissed and pushed them back. Pushed his dragon down, and held it, even as the shaking became almost too much for him to bear.

He couldn't see where he was going. The street spun around him, colored lights lurching sickeningly.

I have to get out of town. No one can see—

Jasper cried out as another soul-wrenching shudder gripped him. He ran. When the lights turned into shadows, and the right angles of buildings turned into the curves and sharp edges of snow and rock, he let go.

Jasper's dragon burst out of him. His claws dug into the snow, screeching on hard rock, and then he was airborne, the icy wind billowing under his wings. He *flew*.

He gained height quickly, flying strong, wings battering the air. The mountains swung below him, cold and remote. The peaks and valleys of his childhood. The dragon knew every one of them, every hidden cave and secret ice-melt stream. His territory. His home. Except— who was he? The dragon, or the man?

The dragon screamed into the night. Jasper screamed with it, and the sound seemed to shock him awake.

He was still there. He was still *himself.* This was just a shift. Like he'd done tens of thousands of times before.

There… Twinkling lights filled a valley, like someone had spilled jewels into the mountain and they had trickled down the slopes to pool together in one beautiful, glimmering pile. Pine Valley. A hundred thousand lights, a thousand human souls— and one of them called to him, so sweet and so longing that his heart ached with being apart from her.

His mate was down there. Abigail. Sweet, prickly, beautiful— and she had sent him away.

His dragon screamed again as he remembered how she had pulled away from him. All he'd wanted was to hold her, help her. He would have stayed out of the way while she called her manager, but she didn't want that. Didn't want *him.* She had pushed him away— she had—

The dragon was huge, and powerful, but its soul ran on instinct. Deep inside it, Jasper's human self frowned. He knew there was more to what had just happened than simple rejection.

But the dragon was in charge now. When he was in human form, he'd ignored his dragon's desire to fly away with Abigail, and now it was too late. The dragon's fiery soul was cracking. Whatever his human self had to say was lost in the dragon's roar.

Jasper turned away from the glittering town, and flew into the night.

13

ABIGAIL

Abigail's chest ached.

Mr. Bell had responded to her call with all the frenzied speed of a person determined to find someone else to blame for the situation. He had bustled up in record time, puffed full of disbelief that the situation was as bad a she had described, and more than ready to tear her down for wasting his time. When he saw the water dripping down the walls and ceiling, his eyes had narrowed to angry slits.

Then, to her surprise, he'd clambered up into the crawlspace himself to see where the water was coming in. His discovery that the nephew he'd employed to set up the Christmas display had attached it by driving nails through the roof had stoked his fury to boiling point— but he hadn't directed it at Abigail.

Instead, Mr. Bell had clapped her on the shoulder, and actually thanked her for reporting the problem.

She watched him stump off, feeling like her insides had been scooped out. He hadn't yelled at her. He hadn't even growled. She'd been ready for either— both— waiting on edge for the situation to devolve into painful accusations and recriminations.

But… nothing. And instead of feeling relieved, Abigail felt sick. She had freaked out for nothing. Jasper probably thought she was a psycho, and he was right.

What the hell was wrong with her?

She wrapped her arms around herself and hurried out into the square. It was past two in the morning, and town was empty; even most of the Christmas lights had been switched off. If she squinted, she could pretend it was only the streetlights illuminating the cold square. Pretend that it wasn't Christmas at all.

Abigail stuffed her hands deeper into her pockets. There was no sign of Jasper.

Like you really thought he'd stick around, she berated herself. It had been an hour since she told him to leave. Why the hell would he have stayed? *Face it. You ruined this, just like you ruin everything.*

Her fingers brushed against something deep in her coat pocket. Her cell phone. For just a moment, she considered calling him. They had exchanged numbers that morning.

God, was it only this morning? Abigail shook her head. It felt like eternity ago. That's what happens when you screw everything up. The world splits into before— and after, when you can't change anything.

She left her phone in her pocket, telling herself there was no point calling him; he was probably halfway back to his family's home by now.

Abigail shivered as a lingering drop of snowmelt made its way down her neck. She sighed. The real reason she wasn't calling him was that she was afraid. She'd driven him away; what if he didn't even pick up the phone?

Better not to know, than to confirm that he didn't want anything to do with her.

24 DECEMBER

CHRISTMAS EVE

For the first few moments after she woke up, Abigail didn't know what was wrong. Then she rolled over and opened her eyes.

Oh.

She was alone in bed. That was it.

Abigail sat up, blinking until her eyes cleared. Her alarm was blaring, and she turned it off, resisting the urge to throw it across the room.

She'd only woken up with Jasper beside her three times. And she'd known the whole time, every minute of every day, that it was going to end badly. And now it had. So why was she so upset?

Jasper's face flashed into her mind. The look in his eyes when she told him to leave, like she'd slapped him. The way he'd marched off, not even looking back at her, as though he was desperate to get away from her.

Bitterness rose up in her throat. Of course he wouldn't look back. Not after the way you talked to him. He probably thinks you're a psycho. Freaking out about your stupid workplace—

Her skin flushed cold. The shop. She gritted her teeth and fisted her hands so hard her knuckles went white, trying to force the wave of anxiety back. See? Freaking out. Like a psycho.

Abigail took a deep breath, reminding herself that she had called Mr. Bell after Jasper left. You mean, after you drove him away. She winced.

She quickly checked her phone. No messages. Nothing from Mr. Bell, which meant she should hurry and get in to work as usual.

And nothing from Jasper.

She waited until she had herself mostly under control, and then stomped through to the bathroom and turned the shower on. The water blasted against her head and shoulders, knocking her thoughts even further out of order.

Nothing about this is a surprise. You knew it wasn't going to last, and you knew you were going to be the reason it all fell to pieces. So just deal with it. You know what to do. Back into the routine. Back to work. Forget all about—

Abigail banged her forehead against the shower wall. *Damn it, damn it, damn it…*

By the time she stepped out of the shower, skin stinging from the hot water, her mind was a boiling fog of unhappiness. Her only saving grace was that with no message from management, she had to assume work was open. If the shop was closed today… hell, she didn't know what she would do.

She took a deep breath. "As if Mr. Bell would ever close the store on Christmas Eve," she reassured herself. Her voice sounded thin in the steaming bathroom and she shook her head. Christmas was their top sales month. Even if the roof completely disintegrated, Mr. Bell would have her and Carol hand-selling mass-produced knick-knacks from the side of the road. It was going to be fine. Everything was going to be fine.

Except her and Jasper. Which she shouldn't even be upset about. She'd only known him for a few days. It wasn't a big deal. Shit.

As she scrubbed herself dry, something caught the corner of her eye. Abigail sighed. Part of her was glad of the distraction, but part of her...

"Why didn't I throw you away that first night?" she grumbled at the kitten plushie she had "rescued" from the shop roof the night she met Jasper. It was sitting on top of the washer, which was pushed into an out-of-the-way corner while it wasn't in use.

A gentle cycle in her washer, a few days drip-drying in the shower and half an hour under her hairdryer had somehow made it look even more pathetic. Its fur was fluffy, but its stuffing had shrunk, giving it a floppy, depressed look. Plus, it still only had the one eye... and she hadn't gotten around to sewing its leg back on.

Abigail's stomach flipped over as she wondered briefly if Jasper had seen it one of the nights he'd been here— God, that would have been embarrassing.

She shook herself. *As if that matters now. You're probably never going to see him again.*

She pulled her clothes on quickly. The toy should have gone straight in the garbage. She didn't know what she was thinking, trying to fix it up. She snatched it up and marched back through to the kitchenette.

Abigail paused, holding the kitten plushie over the garbage bin. One bead-eye glittered back at her. Her chest twisted.

"Damn it," she muttered, and threw the toy onto the countertop. It skidded to stop next to her handbag. "I can't even throw out a stupid toy? What the hell is wrong with me?"

She checked the clock. Half an hour to opening… if the shop was going to open again. Anxiety gnawed at her stomach.

"What do you mean, the shop isn't opening today?"

Abigail pulled her scarf tighter around her neck, trying to block out the icy wind that was whipping through the town square. Mr. Bell huffed at her, his white cloud of breath racing away on the air. He gestured up at the shop, where bright DO NOT CROSS streamers had been plastered over the Christmas tinsel.

"Isn't safe, Abby-babby." Abigail winced at the nickname, but Mr. Bell chuckled to himself, not noticing. "We've been completely banned from setting foot in the place until the builders can get in properly and check it out."

"But it's Christmas Eve!"

Mr. Bell laughed again and slapped Abigail on the shoulder. "Would you believe it! My first Christmas Eve off in twenty years." He sighed happily and patted Abigail on the shoulder again grinning. "All because you were working late, eh? That deserves a bonus! Now, stop sulking, and enjoy your day off!"

He stuck his hands in his pockets and walked off, whistling. Abigail stared after him. She wasn't imagining it. Mr. Bell, who in all the time she'd worked for him seemed to only have two emotional settings— "grumpy" and "furious"— was actually whistling. And when he'd smiled at her, she didn't have the feeling he was holding himself back from biting her head off.

Have I wandered into the Twilight Zone? Abigail wondered, and shivered. Twilight Zone or not, it was still Christmas Eve. And she wasn't going to wait around for it to get any worse.

Her first stop was the grocery store. What with Jasper— she grimaced— well, what with everything, she hadn't managed to do her usual prep shopping earlier in the week. If she kept her head down, she didn't have to see all the shoppers on their last-minute food runs. That didn't save her from hearing them, though. Parents, grandparents, children— all half-frazzled and half-drunk with the joy of the season.

In the frozen section, Abigail grabbed blindly at ready-meals, not bothering to check what she was piling into her basket. So long as it was food, that was good enough.

There was a big display of red wine at the end of the aisle. The bottles had little packets of mulling spices taped to their necks. Abigail swallowed.

No. I'm not going back to that so-called solution. My Christmas System is best when it doesn't include getting blind drunk. Anyway... She blinked hard. Mulled wine just made her think of Jasper, now, and going sledding with those adorable dogs. She put her head down and headed for the checkouts.

Voices pressed in on her as she waited in line. She looked down, focusing on the armful of frozen meals in her basket, but couldn't help overhearing other shoppers' conversations. She was almost at the front of the queue when the older woman in front of her gave a cry of delight and reached past her to greet someone further back.

"Jeanine! Shopping again?"

Abigail could practically feel the other woman's smile lasering into the back of her head. "Yes! You know, we had almost given up hope that Jared would be home for Christmas, but guess who turned up this morning?"

"Oh, how lovely! You'll have the whole family together!"

The shopping basket handle was cutting into Abigail's fingers.

"I was worried for a while that he wouldn't come, how silly of me! Jared loves his family far too much to leave us all alone at Christmas. And you should just *see* the presents he's brought…"

Abigail felt like her head was in a vice. She glanced up at the front of the queue. "The checkout's free," she muttered, hoping the older woman would take the hint and hurry to the counter. Her tongue felt thick and clumsy, and her ears were buzzing.

If I have to listen to another minute of happy families, I'm going to scream, she thought desperately.

"Oh— dear?" Someone tapped her shoulder. "Are you all right? You're looking a little peaky."

Abigail looked up. The older woman was staring into her face, looking concerned.

"I'm fine," Abigail said quickly. Her voice was more of a snarl, and she had to clear her throat. *Damn it. This is why I always do my shopping early…* "Look, there's a checkout free up there—"

"You take my space, dear, while I talk to my friend."

Who does that woman think she is? Abigail fumed to herself as she stalked down the cold streets. Rubbing it in everyone's faces that, oh, her husband or son or whatever would travel a thousand miles to see her for Christmas— and Mr. Bell? I've worked for him for how many years, and he's—

She came to a stop outside her apartment building, suddenly exhausted. *He's giving me a day off. Which most people would see as a good thing. And that woman at the shop was just excited. And she let you cut ahead in line.* Her shoulders slumped. *She was just excited. And Mr. Bell was excited, too. He's worked every Christmas Eve same as you have. He's probably looking forward to spending it… with his family…*

All the events of the last twenty-four hours came crashing down on her like an avalanche, thick and heavy and suffocating. She pushed through the front door and sagged against the inside wall, panting. Was this really what she'd turned into? Someone who saw the worst in people, even when they'd done nothing but be nice to her?

This is why you have the System, she reminded herself, trying to corral her fluttering emotions. *The Christmas System. Work, and sleep, and don't talk to anyone, don't see anyone, because you're not worth being around at Christmas.*

A hole opened up in her chest, which was stupid, because she *knew* all of this. Telling it to herself was meant to calm her down. Make her understand she had everything under control. Not make her feel like her body was about to split into a million pieces.

Just keep yourself out of the way. That's the best option. That way no one gets disappointed.

She took a shaky breath and fumbled with the latch on her mailbox.

You don't get disappointed when no one shows up for you. And no one else gets disappointed, when they see you.

The mailbox clattered open. Why was she even bothering? She wasn't expecting anything. She'd cancelled all her subscriptions over the holidays, and it wasn't like she got any mail that wasn't someone trying to sell her something. *No one wants to put up with you. You don't deserve anyone.*

She paused, her heart pounding her in ears. There *was* something in her mailbox. A piece of white card.

Probably a message from the landlord, she told herself, but something fluttered in her chest. Before she could stop herself, she reached up.

She was still wearing her gloves. Her fingers shouldn't have tingled as she picked up the card, not unless she was in the early stages of frostbite. But they did. And when she saw what it was, her breath caught in her throat.

Jasper's Christmas card.

A troupe of huskies grinned up at her from the front of the card, cheery Christmas-cracker hats perched on their heads. *Merry Christmas!* was scrawled in tinsel underneath them, and behind them, the mountains went on forever.

Her fingers tightened. She didn't want to turn it over. No. She did, and she didn't. Her hand trembled with tension.

Just read it. What's the worst that can happen?

Before she could answer her own question, she flipped the card over and all the breath left her body.

Dear Abigail,

I know you don't like Christmas. But I'm hoping that by the time this arrives, I've managed to bring you around. And that I'm watching you read this, waiting for you to scowl at me, with that little smile that means you're not really mad. Merry Christmas.

All my love,

Jasper

The rest of the world disappeared. Abigail read the postcard again, frantically, half-expecting the words to disappear if she looked at them too closely. But they didn't. This wasn't a dream. It was real.

And even though it wasn't a dream, she couldn't help glancing over her shoulder. Jasper wasn't there, of course. He wasn't watching her read his card, like he'd wanted to be. Abigail's chest twisted.

I really fucked that up, huh?

She groaned and banged her head against the rack of mailboxes. She knew she shouldn't have read the card. It was just another reminder of how everything she touched went wrong.

The metal mailboxes were cool against her forehead. She closed her eyes. *I'm hoping that by the time this arrives, I've managed to bring you around…* And, the truth was, he almost had. All those perfect dates. The terrible egg-nog. Ice-skating under the stars. And the dogsledding, that magical adventure in the glittering midnight forest. Mulled wine and stew in front of a frozen lake.

She frowned. Perfect dates? They'd all turned out well, but… that egg-nog had been *revolting.* And she'd fallen asleep on the sled-ride. She couldn't imagine that had been part of Jasper's plan.

Just like discovering the roof about to fall in wasn't part of yours.

Abigail's chest went tight. She'd let that one discovery set off an avalanche in her mind, turning a setback into a disaster. As though— she winced.

Admit it. You've been waiting for something to go wrong the whole week, and the moment it did, you ran with it. It was almost a relief, wasn't it? You saw the worst possible outcome, and you kicked it off. You set off that avalanche.

But it didn't feel like relief, now. She didn't feel like she'd escaped disaster, like she'd found a way to protect herself from being hurt. She felt empty.

Abigail looked down at the postcard in her hand. Jasper's first few attempts to reach out to her hadn't been flawless, but he hadn't let that frighten him off. So even though her first attempt to reach back had gone so wrong, maybe… just maybe…

Her skin flushed hot and cold. She couldn't do this. A lifetime of experience couldn't be wrong, could it? It was pointless to hope that anyone wanted her at Christmas. She could reach out all she wanted, and be left to fall alone.

She gripped the postcard so hard it bent in her fingers. Biting her lip, Abigail carefully smoothed it out.

She had spent the last ten years making sure she didn't have to reach out to anybody. She looked after herself, and didn't need anyone else.

She survived, but that was all. And Jasper had shown her there was more to life than just surviving.

14

JASPER

The dragon had been flying all night, until its wings ached with the cold. As dawn rose pink and gold over the mountains, it turned back. Back towards its—

Home? No. It wasn't home anymore.

The knowledge ripped through the dragon's body. It was unmoored. Unanchored. Even the golden song of its hoard, deep in the mountains, didn't steady it. What use was a hoard, with no mate to share it with?

Abigail.

Somewhere deep inside the dragon, Jasper opened his eyes. He felt as though he had slept for a thousand years, lost in the deep currents of his dragon's agony. Slowly, piece by piece, he pulled himself to the surface.

How long was I under? He looked out through his dragon's eyes. The sky was thick with heavy cloud, but night's darkness was drawing away; in the distance, a smudge of pink-gold hinted at the sun's arrival. Morning. But what morning? Christmas Eve, or…

Does it matter? The dragon shuddered again. It had its own opinions on the matter, Jasper knew. But as for himself… he wasn't sure whether he cared one way or another. Before he'd met Abigail, he'd planned to stay human, but now…

He would have his family, either way. Live in the mountains as a dragon. See Cole grow up. Maybe that was best. What was the point of being human, now that Abigail had rejected him?

Abigail. It hurt to think her name. Hurt in a way that was almost pleasure, bright and icy-sharp. His dragon could sense her presence, even from this distance, and that hurt, too. She glittered like a star in the snow, all sharp smiles and pointy edges that he'd almost managed to make his way past. Almost. Not close enough.

The dragon's wings drooped. It was weary, now, after its broken flight through the darkness. Head heavy, it descended into the thick clouds. Even if it had no home, it still needed to—

The trees came up faster than Jasper or the dragon had expected, black knives lancing up through the cloud. Branches cracked, trunks splintered, and the dragon roared in pain as it crashed to the ground.

Jasper didn't know where he was. The world spun around him, broken trees and hard snow and low, suffocating cloud. The dragon dropped its head onto the icy ground. Plumes of white vapor streamed from its nostrils.

The dragon could feel the others' voices searching for it. They must have felt his pain— Opal, Hank, even tiny Cole. Their minds were like jeweled suns, seeking his out.

It closed its mind to them. Deep inside it, Jasper did the same.

He was alone.

15

ABIGAIL

Abigail gripped the steering wheel so tightly that her knuckles were white.

Maybe it was pointless, and hopeless, and reckless and stupid and a terrible idea in so many ways— but she was going to do it. Even if she knocked on his door and he didn't answer. Even if he sent her away.

She'd had all the chances in the world to change her mind. Putting chains on the tires of her crappy old car had been a mission and a half; at any point, she could have given up. But she hadn't. Sweaty and greasy, she'd pulled out of the apartment garage with her stomach in knots.

She was going to find Jasper.

The streets were busy. That gave her more chances to back out. Every excruciating inch was another opportunity for her to decide this was all a mistake, that reaching out like this was no better than throwing herself off into thin air with no parachute. She rapped her fingers on the steering wheel. She didn't *want* all these chances to change her mind.

Because you're afraid you might take one of them.

That was why she had decided to go in person, rather than call on the phone. A phone call could be missed; face-to-face, there was no way to hide.

At last, an opening appeared in the traffic. She edged forward, heaving a sigh of relief. No escape now. She was stuck here until the great traffic-beast spat her out on the mountain road a few blocks away. And then she was going to find Jasper. He'd told her where he was staying; one of the private lodges, up one of the private roads. She'd never explored that far into the mountains, but now she had a reason to ignore the *Restricted Access* signs. And when she got there…

Christmas Eve. Abigail's heart leapt into her throat. Jasper loved Christmas. And she was going to go up there and beg for him to take her back, empty-handed? What was she thinking?

A shop up ahead caught her eye. It wasn't the sort of place she usually went, but today— today, it might just be perfect. Horns blaring around her, Abigail inched into a parking space and raced inside.

Half an hour later, she was on the mountain road. The town traffic had dragged at her patience, but out here, it was like a weight had lifted from her shoulders. There were only a few other cars on the road, and they soon disappeared ahead of her. It was like she was alone in the mountains; just her, her crotchety old car, and the parcel burning a hole in her jacket pocket.

The roads had all been cleared since the last snow, but she was still glad of the chains as she drove deeper into the mountains. Her car barely had four-wheel drive, and— now that she came to think of it— she hadn't actually told anyone she was heading out here…

She checked her phone. One bar of signal.

Stop it. You're not backing out, remember?

She reminded herself of this again when she pulled to a stop in front of the gate that led onto the Heartwells' private road. It was closed— but not locked, as she discovered when she trudged out to check it. She drove through, and then stopped to close the gate after her. Her skin prickled.

You're not doing anything wrong. You're visiting a, a friend. And it's not like the gate was locked, or anything.

She looked around, wrapping her arms around herself. It was a gray, dull day. Heavy clouds smothered the peaks. Maybe if it was clear, she would have been able to see up to the Heartwell lodge, but instead she felt like she was standing under a dome of fog. She shivered.

I hope Jasper has a fire going, she thought, and immediately shook her head. If he even wants to see you.

"Well, I'm not going to find out by standing around here," she said out loud, and turned to trudge back to the car.

A noise stopped her.

Abigail froze, ears pricked. *What was that?* It wasn't the creak of ice-bound trees, or the crash of snow falling from an overhand or branch. It had sounded almost like some sort of animal. Like a groan.

Are there bears around here? was her first thought, and then: Should I run?

But she didn't move. Whatever that noise was… it wasn't like anything she had ever heard, but she wasn't afraid. And she wanted to know what had made it.

She turned away from the car. Silence. The only noise was her footsteps as she took one, two steps forward. There was a stand of pines near the side of the road, thickening to dense forest that swept up the hillside beyond. But there was something wrong. The trees seemed to thin out again partway up the hill. And while most of the trees were thickly blanketed with snow, the branches around that one spot were bare. Like something had shaken all the snow off them.

Abigail waited. The only things she could hear were her own breath, and the crunch of snow underfoot. She realized she was still walking forward and forced herself to stop. What was she doing, wandering into a forest in the middle of nowhere? If one of those trees dumped its load of snow on her, that would be it. She'd be dead of hypothermia long before anyone noticed she was missing.

She bit her lip. No more noises. But she hadn't heard it the last time until she'd spoken out loud to herself. So, maybe— well, maybe it was an echo, but she had to be sure either way—

"Hello?" she called out.

The forest sighed back. Abigail swayed on her feet. She *had* heard it. Whatever it was. A sigh, a groan— like something in pain. Or some*one*.

The hairs on the backs of her arms stood on end, even under all her layers of clothing. Whatever it was, she wasn't going to leave here without investigating further.

She made her way slowly through the trees, choosing each step with care. She didn't dare call out again, in case the sound of her voice disturbed any of the snow piled up on the tree branches. Skin prickling with anticipation, she picked her way up the hill.

It was easy to tell when she was getting close. Shattered branches covered the ground, and even some of the massive pine trunks were broken off. *It's like something huge fell out of the sky,* Abigail thought to herself. *Has a plane crashed? Wouldn't I have heard about that on the news, though?*

Except she didn't listen to the news. Not at Christmas. She would have missed—

Abigail frowned. No. Even if I missed a news bulletin, I would have seen search and rescue teams on the road. There would have been something. This is…

She squeezed around a thick layer of brush and gasped. *This is something else.*

For a moment, her mind refused to believe what it was seeing. The— *creature*— was immense, its body at least the length of a bus and its tail stretching out even longer behind it. And its wings. It had wings. And scales. And a long, lizard-like head with a line of ridges that ran from behind its nostrils up over its eyes, becoming thicker and harder-looking as they went down its massive back.

The creature's eyes were closed, and the skin of its eyelids looked strangely delicate next to the clear power and strength of the rest of it.

Not a creature. A dragon. She didn't have any other word for it and her mind rebelled against it— it was impossible— but there it was. A dragon, crash-landed in the snowy mountains above her home.

Its scales gleamed bright against the white snow and dark trees, a shimmering gold-red-orange that danced like flames.

"This can't be real," Abigail whispered, so quietly she could barely hear the words.

The dragon opened its eyes.

Abigail felt as though she was floating. The dragon's eyes were the same colors as its scales, but filled with liquid fire. Gold and red and orange, strange and magical and— *familiar*.

Her thought broke off as the dragon began to move. Its eyes were locked on to hers, and it moved slowly, as though it was trying not to frighten her. It pulled its legs back and shifted its weight until it was crouching Sphinx-like in the broken mess of trees and snow.

Abigail was so entranced, she almost forgot to breathe. She was drowning in the dragon's eyes. Drowning and flying at the same time, her whole body alight with wonder.

The dragon hissed with pain, a sharp, bitten-back noise. Abigail stiffened, but didn't retreat. She immediately saw what was wrong. One of the dragon's wings was caught on a broken branch in such a way that it couldn't pull it free.

"Stay where you are," Abigail said at once. She didn't bother to wonder whether it could understand her. It must have, anyway, because it stayed frozen in place as she clambered over broken trees and snowdrifts to grab hold of the splintered branch. "Hold still— I'll try not to hurt you, but…"

She yanked on the branch. Frozen wood cracked and splintered, and she managed to haul it away enough that the dragon could hitch its wing back. She watched, panting, as it folded its wing awkwardly against its side. It hadn't taken its eyes off her the whole time.

Abigail scrambled backwards until she was on solid ground again. The dragon swung its massive head around, following her. She still wasn't scared. She thought she probably should be— if not of the massive mythological creature in front of her, then the possibility that this was all a hallucination, and she was seriously ill or injured. But she wasn't.

Because she knew those eyes. Gold and red and orange, like looking into the heart of a fire. Like embers, burning with passion.

This is impossible. But…

"Jasper?" she breathed.

She bit her lip the moment the word was out. *Of all the stupid ideas to enter your head—*

The dragon— it couldn't be Jasper, that was stupid, that was the most ridiculous thing she'd ever heard— the dragon pushed itself up on legs the size of tree-trunks. When it stood up, she could see the damage from its crash into the trees, a thousand cuts and grazes. Some small. Some not so small.

"You're hurt," she gasped as the dragon stumbled. It lowered its head until its eyes were level with hers, only a few feet away. Its mouth was just open enough that she could see its long, curved teeth.

But that wasn't what caught her attention. There was a cut on the dragon's lip, giving it a cruel-looking sneer. A broken splinter of wood was jammed into the end of the cut.

Abigail reached out automatically, then hesitated. The dragon's breath flowed over her, warm and spicy-smelling. She took a deep breath. *Forget hypothermia. If this goes wrong, you're going to be burned to a crisp.*

Her gloves were too thick and clumsy. She would have to do it bare-handed.

"This is *definitely* going to hurt," she warned the dragon after she had stripped off her gloves, and took hold of the splinter. As gently as she could, she began to ease it out.

The dragon's breath surrounded her, and she could feel its eyes on her, so strange and so strangely familiar.

"Here—just a little more—" The dragon was tense, its breath coming in sharp puffs of spice-scented fog. The splinter was longer than she had expected, and she winced in sympathy as she pulled it slowly from the dragon's lip. "Almost there—"

Without thinking, she raised her other hand to steady herself against the dragon's snout. A violent shudder went through the dragon, almost throwing Abigail to the ground. The splinter flew out of her hand and onto the snow, but the dragon didn't stop shaking— it was shimmering, almost as though its whole shape was changing—

Light filled the clearing. She had grabbed on to the dragon when it started shaking but it wasn't a dragon anymore. There weren't scales under her palms, there was skin. Her fingers tangled in curling hair.

She fell to her knees and he fell with her. Not a dragon.

"Jasper," she gasped, staring up at him. The dragon's eyes gazed back at her, from Jasper's face. Red and gold and burning and…

I was right. It is Jasper. The dragon— how is this possible?

"Abigail—" Jasper's voice was choked. His face was scratched, his hair tousled with snow and twigs, but he was staring at her like she was the most precious thing in the world.

"How— what—" Abigail had too many questions. Then Jasper's arms closed around her and all her questions dissolved. He kissed her hungrily, desperately, and Abigail clung to him, drinking him in. His kisses. His touch. His tangled hair, the smooth lines of his back under her hands— was he naked?

His injuries. She'd seen the cut on his face, still— was he—

Abigail was still gathering her thoughts when Jasper groaned and sagged against her. She braced against him, pushing them both to kneel upright. Jasper's head lolled on her shoulder.

"Jasper!"

"'m alright," he muttered, his voice slurred. "I…"

He collapsed against her, too heavy for her to hold. They both fell to their knees.

16

JASPER

He meant to say more. He was fine, he was dandy, everything was wonderful… but the words didn't make it out of his mouth. They barely made it through his head. Everything was fuzzy. And cold.

"You're naked and bleeding in the snow on a mountainside in the middle of *nowhere.*"

Jasper grinned into Abigail's shoulder. She sounded so annoyed. "'s alright," he managed to croak. "'s not a problem."

Her irritated *tsk* warmed his heart. Which was good, because a lot of the rest of him was really cold. Really, really cold.

"And you're a dragon. And… I need to get you back to the car," Abigail muttered. Probably to herself. But Jasper agreed. Car. That was a good idea.

He tried to help as she put his arm over her shoulder and led him back down the hillside, but his foots weren't walking properly. Feets. Feet. Legs. Wings. *No!* No wings. If he couldn't walk he *definitely* couldn't fly. Also, he would probably squish Abigail if he shifted now. That would be bad. That would be *so* bad.

Something smacked into his stomach and Jasper looked down. A car? He was sure he hadn't left the car here. "Wassat?"

"My shitty car," Abigail said. Her voice seemed to be floating somewhere under his left elbow. He was sure she didn't used to be that short. Except— his elbow was higher than it usually was. Because it was on her shoulder! He remembered now.

He tried to explain his line of reasoning to Abigail as she tipped him into the passenger seat, but wasn't sure if he did it very well.

Warm air blasted him in the face. "At least the heating's working," Abigail muttered from the driver's seat. He gazed across at her. She was so beautiful. Especially when she was frowning at him like that. And biting her lip. "Your place is further up this road, right?"

He nodded. "Mmm," he said, eloquently, and dozed off. Abigail. Car. His place. Good.

Jasper jerked awake. "Nrrr," he said urgently. "Turn off here."

"Here?" The car slowed down and Jasper felt Abigail tap him on the cheek. "Are you even awake?"

"Yes," Jasper insisted. He blinked until his eyes focused in on her. This was important. She could *not* drive straight up to the Heartwell lodge. That would be… awkward. Terrible. All the bad things.

Abigail raised her eyebrows. "Am I going to take the word of a naked, half-frozen man-dragon, to turn down this road towards a house that may exist only in his raving dreams… or the proof of my own eyes, which can definitely see a house up ahead here?" She pointed and Jasper groaned. The Heartwell lodge was clearly visible a few miles up the road.

He turned to Abigail, summoning his most imploring face. "Raving man-dragon. Please."

Abigail squeezed her eyes shut. "Fine," she grumbled, and hauled on the wheel. Gravel crunched under the car wheels as they started down the side-road.

That's good, Jasper thought. Take her home. Proper home. No Cole jumping on her. Home… hoard…

He reached out one hand and put it on her thigh, reassuring himself she was still there. She felt hot, even through her pants. Or maybe he was cold still? Something to think about. Later. After a short nap…

Jasper hadn't thought ahead enough to wonder what to expect when he and Abigail reached his cottage. But whatever he might have expected, it wasn't waking up half-in a steaming hot bath. He flailed.

"Hey! Watch it!" Abigail squeaked. "Jeez, you're heavy enough even without— just get in, will you?"

Jasper paused. His mind was still cotton-candy-fuzzy, but he was awake enough to take account of where he was. Inside. Hot bath. Abigail's arms under his armpits, lowering him into bath.

"Mmm," he moaned, and relaxed down into the tub. "'s good."

"I should hope so. You're freezing, it's all I could think of…"

Jasper's dragon tensed. Abigail's voice was brittle with worry. He turned around, holding onto the edge of the bath and seeking out his mate's face.

She met his eyes and sat down on the floor with a thud, reaching over the edge of the tub to hug his shoulders. He could feel her muscles shaking.

"Abigail…" he murmured. Her name didn't hurt to think or say anymore. It sat like an ember in the very center of his heart, warming his soul.

"You wouldn't wake up," she whispered into his shoulder. "You were so cold, and you were bleeding— and then you weren't bleeding, and it looked like all your cuts were, were gone, but you were even colder…"

And you dragged me out of the car and in here, terrified out of your mind. Jasper kissed her neck until she stopped shaking, and then lifted her chin off his shoulder. "You did exactly the right thing," he reassured her. It wasn't the hot bath that was sending energy through his veins, though. It was *her.* Just her, being here, with him.

It was almost perfect. Jasper's mind was clearing. "There's only one other thing I need right now," he said, his voice husky.

"Anything— hey!" Abigail protested as he looped his arms around her and started to pull her over the side of the tub. "I'm still wearing all my clothes!"

Jasper kissed her. "I know." He rose up, pressing his chest against hers— and leaned backwards, pulling her with him.

"You—" Abigail put her hands on his chest, pushing him away, and an adorable line appeared between her eyebrows. "Is this a…"

Her voice trailed away and she bit her lower lip.

"Go on," urged Jasper, his heart racing. She'd seen him. She'd seen him as a dragon, and she had seen him shift. He wanted to hear her say it.

Abigail's cheeks went pink. "I…" She groaned and ducked her head. "God, this sounds so stupid.

I thought you were a dragon. But I must have been dreaming, or hallucinating from the shock—just like I thought you were injured worse than you actually are…"

Jasper a finger under her chin and lifted her head back up. "You weren't dreaming or hallucinating," he murmured. Abigail's eyes went wide, and inside him, Jasper's dragon preened. "I can turn into a dragon."

"Bullshit."

Jasper laughed out loud. "Bullshit? You *saw* it."

"I saw—" Abigail's face had been tense with self-doubt, but now it cleared. Her eyes shone. "I *did* see it. You were a dragon, and then you turned into… into you. It was amazing. Magical."

She relaxed against him, and Jasper took advantage of her inattention to scoop her up and pull her on top of himself in the bath. She shrieked and splashed until he pacified her with a passionate kiss.

"God dammit," she grumbled into his lips. "You couldn't have waited for me to get undressed?"

"No." Jasper felt as though sunlight was running through his veins. He worked his way under Abigail's jacket and sweater until his fingers found her skin, warm and soft and wonderful. "There wasn't time." He kissed her again. "I needed you. I *need* you. Here. Right now." Another kiss. "No time to lose."

Abigail's cheeks were even pinker now. Droplets of water clung to her eyelashes like tiny diamonds. She had never looked more beautiful. "You needed me? Is that a… a dragon thing?"

Jasper stroked her lower back, drawing small circles with his palm. "Partly," he admitted. He nipped her lower lip before she could bite down on it. "Mostly, I didn't want to spend another moment without you in my arms."

He lay back in the bathtub, the water lapping around his chest. Abigail moved with him, lying with her head resting on his shoulder. Jasper could already feel the strength returning to his limbs. And… other places.

Was it only hours ago that he'd given up hope? And now everything his heart desired was here, in his arms.

"I was lost, and you found me. You brought me back," he murmured.

He looked down at his precious, beautiful Abigail. His mate. Her jacket, soaking wet and heavy, covered them both like a blanket; under it she was wearing sensible pants and a warm knit sweater. The ends of her hair were wet, floating on the surface of the water like delicate seaweed. And her face was pale.

"What's wrong?" he asked, sweeping a wet strand of hair behind her ear. Abigail squeezed her eyes shut briefly.

"I almost didn't come," she admitted in a whisper. "I thought— after last night— when I freaked out at you… you wouldn't want anything to do with me."

Jasper's arms tightened around her of their own accord. "Never," he said firmly. "And, remember. You're not the only one who freaked out."

"I…" Abigail grimaced and pushed herself upright. The bath was big enough so that they could both sit in it comfortably; Jasper waited as she settled herself at the other end, then reached out for her hand. She took his immediately. "I came here to apologize, and explain, and I— wait." Her eyes searched his, suddenly tense. "You freaked out, too? Is that why… Oh, God." She seemed to crumple in on herself. "Was that because of me? You getting hurt?"

Guilt lanced across her face. Jasper leaned forward, cupping her cheek. The need to reassure her tangled with the truth on his lips, tying his tongue in knots.

Abigail covered his hand with her own and took a deep breath. "It is, isn't it? I drove you off, and you turned into a dragon and… hurt yourself. It's all my fault."

"No. No, Abigail, it's not like that." Jasper pulled her hand to his lips and kissed it. She looked so small and lost. He needed to fix that. "It's— it's another dragon thing. Usually, I'm in balance with my dragon. I can control when I shift. But I'm… I'm not completely well, at the moment."

"You're sick?"

"Not quite." Jasper ran his thumb over Abigail's knuckles, staring deep into her eyes. "This Christmas is a… well, it was always going to be a difficult time for me."

"And I made it worse." Abigail's mouth went tight and she looked away.

"No. You made it better. So much better than I ever could have imagined. What happened last night was…" Jasper hunted for a way to explain that wasn't too much, too fast. Abigail looked like she was on the edge of breaking down already. He couldn't push her over the edge. "My dragon isn't the sharpest spoon in the drawer. When it thought you didn't want us anymore, didn't want *me*, it almost broke out. I'm sorry I ran away. It was either that or shift in the middle of town." He paused. "Maybe I should have."

Abigail made a noise that was half-hiccup, half-laughter. "Last night? In the middle of the square? I would have freaked out so hard, I went into orbit." She pulled her hand off her cheek and wiped her face, then sat with both of Jasper's hands in her own, staring hard at the surface of the water.

"I drove you away. No, don't try to tell me I didn't. I drove you away, and I *meant* to. That's what I have to explain."

Jasper's dragon shook inside him. He knew that if he hadn't been holding Abigail's hands, it would have been last night all over again. He pushed his dragon down, reminding it that she had come to him; that she had saved him; that she had seen him shift, and brought him here to care for him, and hadn't run away. The least he and his dragon could do was hear her out without busting the roof off the cottage and disappearing into the sky.

He kept his eyes fixed on Abigail as she spoke. She kept hers fixed on the water.

"I told you I hate Christmas, but I never told you why. When I was a kid, I guess I looked forward to it as much as anyone. Santa, presents, carols, a big Christmas tree with decorations and a star on top… all of that. I was too young to realize those aren't the important things about Christmas.

"After my parents separated, all of that stopped. I figured out pretty quick that Santa didn't exist. The first year, my parents were meant to have Christmas together. I think Mom wanted to give it one last go. One last attempt at playing Happy Families. We did up the whole house, tree, outdoor lights, everything. She spent all the day before cooking."

Jasper's stomach twisted. He could guess what was coming.

"Dad never turned up. Mom couldn't eat anything after she realized he wasn't coming, she said it made her feel sick, so we just threw everything out. Decorations, presents, all of it." Abigail took a deep breath. "The next year, Dad was meant to take me for part of the day, but he didn't. Or any year after that."

She wiped her face again and sniffed. "At first I thought it was my fault. That if I hadn't been there that first Christmas after they separated, if I hadn't asked for so many presents, maybe Mom and Dad would have gotten back together. I mean, obviously that's stupid. They wouldn't have. I figured that out soon enough. But every year that Dad didn't come and see me…

"I learned not to expect anything for Christmas. Or even to *want* to expect anything, because it's so easy to be disappointed even if you tell yourself you're not going to be. So after Mom passed, I moved up here, and I stopped doing Christmas at all. I spent a few years just drinking through the holiday, and then I got it under control. I came up with a system that worked for me. My Christmas System. As much work as I could manage without passing out behind the counter, and then home to sleep. Rinse, repeat. So long as I didn't allow myself any time to think about what I was missing out on, I was fine." She grimaced. "And a good helping of convincing myself it was all bullshit and I wasn't missing out on anything, anyway.

"And then you came along."

"And turned your system upside down." Jasper's heart was breaking for his mate. All those years of thinking she wasn't good enough. "I wish I'd found you years ago. You deserve so much better than that."

"It was the only way I could think of to deal with it. Telling myself that the reason I never tried, never reached out to anyone, was because there was nothing about Christmas that I wanted. Christmas trees, and carols, and presents— as if that was all that Christmas was about." Her voice went small. "I don't think I even realized how unhappy I was, still, until I met you. And once I did, I was so afraid. I thought, this can't last, and what happens when everything goes wrong and you decide I'm not worth the effort anymore?"

Jasper's chest twisted. He thought he understood. "Last night, taking me up to the attic— that was you reaching out. A Christmassy olive branch. And when we found the leak…"

"I couldn't handle it. I thought, this must be it. I tried to break out of my shell, and the universe smacked me down." Abigail bit her lip, but this time Jasper didn't find it adorable. He felt heartsick.

"I didn't know," he said softly, knowing it wasn't enough.

Abigail snorted, blinking hard. "Well, I tried not to go around advertising just how fucked up I am, so that's no surprise."

Jasper squeezed her hands. Everything made sense. Of course she had pulled away— she'd thought everything was falling down around her, so she'd ripped the band-aid off quickly rather than drawing it out. His heart hurt for her. If he'd only told her sooner…

"I knew you were scared," he told her, and she looked up at him, startled. "Not *why*, but I knew something was wrong. There had to be a reason you were so spiky." He smiled sadly at her. "I should have told you I was a dragon shifter earlier. I should have explained you never had to be afraid that I would leave you. But I was scared, too."

Abigail frowned. "You were scared. But you—" She half-laughed and waved one hand, sending droplets flying. "You can turn into a *dragon*. What could you possibly be afraid of?"

"Being alone." Inside him, Jasper's dragon shuddered. This was it. He had to tell her the whole truth. "And losing myself."

Abigail stared at him. Her eyes were red-rimmed, but clear, and filled with concern.

Jasper steeled himself, and told her everything.

17

ABIGAIL

Earlier, Abigail couldn't believe her eyes. Now, she couldn't believe her ears. What Jasper was telling her… it couldn't be true.

She looked deep into his eyes, and bit back a sharp, bitter reply. There was nothing but honesty in his ember-bright gaze.

"But… me?" she said, her voice barely more than a whisper. "What's so special about me?"

"You're my mate," Jasper said simply, his eyes full of love. "My destiny. The one person I'm meant to spend my life with."

"I—" she began, and then reality took hold again. Of course. It wasn't *her* that was important. Not who she was, just what she was. Abigail George, brown-haired human female; not Abigail George, terrible and useless human being.

"Stop it." Jasper's voice was warm and teasing, but with a steel core.

"Stop what?" Abigail said automatically. He couldn't read her mind, could he? She bit her lip.

Jasper reached out and smoothed his thumb over her lower lip until she stopped biting it. "You're telling yourself it isn't true, or you're not good enough. It's not a mistake. You're my mate. I knew it the moment I met you."

Abigail didn't want him to stop stroking her lip, but she couldn't stop herself. "You mean, it's nothing to do with *me*. Just what I look like, or being in the right place at the right time, or—"

"None of that." Jasper stroked her cheek. "The spark was there the moment I saw you, yes. But I didn't know for sure until I got to know you. And once I knew you, how could I do anything else but fall in love with every spiky, grumpy, beautiful bit of you?" His eyes went soft. "You told yourself and everyone else that you hated Christmas, but the first time I ever saw you, you were crawling on a roof to get a present for a little kid. Even when you're hurting, your kindness shines out of you. And the last few days have only confirmed just how strong and wonderful you are."

Abigail's breath caught in her throat. Jasper's eyes were like firelight dancing on gold. No one had ever looked at her like he had. And she—

"But I think I love you," she whispered, the words kindling in her heart and flying from her lips before she knew what she was doing.

Delight shone from Jasper's face. He laughed, pulling her close. "'But'?" he asked, kissing her as water sloshed over the side of the bath. "I love you, too, Abigail. With all of my heart."

"But…" Abigail's mind clutched for some argument, some downside. It must be there, somewhere. The catch. The trick. The penny about to drop. "But… if I love you and you love me…"

Jasper's eyes smoldered into hers. "Then we'll have to live happily ever after," he purred.

All the walls Abigail had built around her heart fell away, dissolving like mist in sunlight. "Oh," she said, feeling light-headed. Then: "Really? Can we?"

Jasper laughed. "Of course. Starting right now." He kissed her again, the touch of his lips against hers like lightning, and then stood up. Water cascaded off his body, making him shimmer in a way that reminded Abigail of his dragon's scales. Light glimmered off his chest and abs, and the long, lean muscles of his thighs. "There's only one thing left. Will you be mine, Abigail? Will you let me claim you as my mate?"

"Didn't you already do that?" Abigail stood up, less sure on her feet in the slippery bath than Jasper was. He steadied her, his hands around her waist.

"There's a ritual." Jasper hesitated, his cheeks tinging pink. "You… uh… you know the stories about how dragons have hoards, right?"

"What, giant piles of gold?" Abigail was joking, but Jasper nodded. "You're not telling me—"

"I have a giant pile of gold in a cave up the mountain," Jasper said quickly, then froze, waiting for her reaction.

Abigail looked up at him, bemused. "And… you're telling me this because…?"

Jasper licked his lips. For the first time, he looked—shy?

Jasper, shy?

"Hey, I just bared my heart to you," she joked, prodding him in the chest. "Come on. Spill."

He grabbed her poking hand and gently bit the tip of her finger. "For me to officially claim you as my mate, we have to lie together on my hoard," he murmured, his voice hoarse.

"Lie together… you mean— ?" Abigail felt her cheeks blaze red. "Like, sleep together?"

"Well I wouldn't advise sleeping on it. I think that would be a bit uncomfortable. But…" He smiled shyly. "Yes. Essentially."

"Oh." Abigail considered. They were already in the bath, and she'd kind of assumed they would stay there for any "lying together", but…

She looked down Jasper's body. God, he was so gorgeous. And he must have been having some of the same thoughts as she was, because his cock was half-hard already.

"You said something about being on a deadline," she said, staring questioningly into his eyes. "Is this claiming something to do with that?"

Jasper nodded. "I don't want to pressure you," he explained. "That's why I waited so long. But if I don't claim my mate by my twenty-fifth birthday, I stop being a shifter. I have to choose whether to be just human, or just dragon— forever."

No! Abigail was surprised by the certainty that shot through her. Jasper was trying to hide it, but it was clear the thought distressed him. The corner of his mouth was twitching. She narrowed her eyes. There was something he still wasn't telling her.

"When is your birthday?" she asked.

Jasper's mouth quirked into a guilty half-smile. "Midnight," he admitted. "Or, if you want to be exact, the first minute of Christmas Day."

"No wonder you're so stuck on Christmas." Abigail groaned and stepped out of the bath. Her coat dragged behind her, sticking to the side of the bath and then her legs. "What are you waiting for? It's early afternoon already, and I'm assuming by 'up in the mountain' you mean your hoard isn't exactly easy to access—"

"No-o," Jasper admitted, following her out of the bath. He grabbed an armful of fluffy towels from a cupboard and handed her one. "You're— you're sure?"

Abigail paused. Any other day, she would have thought his hesitation meant he was trying to back out— but this was Jasper. That couldn't be true.

He'd said he was scared to tell her the truth. Why?

"I'm not going to run away," she said, taking his hand. "I want to do this. To be with you. I don't want you to lose half of yourself just because I made such a hash of things. Especially when I just found out about the other half of you."

"We *both* screwed up," Jasper reminded her, squeezing her hand. He grinned at her. "But you can't go out wearing that. You'll freeze. Come on, I've got dry clothes in the bedroom…"

Jasper's clothes were far too long for Abigail, but she rolled up sleeves and pant legs and buckled on a belt and everything seemed like it was going to stay on. "Right," she said, hanging her coat up to drip dry. "Let's— what's wrong?"

Jasper was standing at the front room window, staring out. "We might have left things a bit late," he said in a low voice.

"What?" Abigail checked the cuckoo clock on the wall. "It's not even three yet, you— oh."

She stood side by side with him, staring out the window. It wasn't dark outside; it was white. Snowstorm white.

The cottage was thickly insulated, and the windows were triple-glazed. If she concentrated, she could just hear the roar of the weather outside. Outside, visibility was so low she could barely see the snow-drifts piling up around and over her car. "Oh," she said again, feeling hollow.

"We can't go out in this." Jasper's voice was carefully level. "You can't. It isn't safe."

Abigail clutched his hand. This couldn't be happening. Not after everything they had been through. "What about you? Could you fly in this?" Jasper nodded, but he looked uncertain. She kept talking before he could change his mind. "If you carry me…"

Half an hour later, they fought their way back into the cottage, defeated by the storm. The snow was coming down so quickly, it had swamped Jasper's wings, preventing him from flying.

Jasper kicked snow from in front of the door and bundled Abigail in ahead of him. She was shivering, and not only from the cold.

Jasper slammed the door shut as another gust of wind sent snow flurrying in after them. He stood there, staring at the shut door, a look of anguish on his face.

Abigail didn't know what to say. She went to him and tentatively put her arms around him. His bare skin was chilled, even though he had only shifted back to human form a few seconds before they came back inside.

"I'm so sorry," she whispered.

Jasper dropped his head onto hers. She felt him breathe out, sharp and hard. "Should have checked the forecast," he said dully, her hair muffling his words. "I was hoping it would snow. But this…"

He fell silent, stroking her hair. His fingers curled against the back of her head and she looked up, searching his eyes.

"I still have you," he said softly. "That's more than I could have dreamed of."

"But without the mate bond— if we can't make it official…" Abigail gulped. The fire in Jasper's eyes was so low, she was worried the storm had almost quenched it. "You'll lose your dragon."

"But I'll still have you."

Abigail swallowed again. She wasn't enough, she knew, not compared to all the magic he was losing. And it was the magic that had brought them together anyway, wasn't it? Without that—

"Abigail." Jasper's voice was tinged with tired amusement. "Stop it. You're more than enough. You're everything." He kissed her, passionately, hungrily. "My love," he murmured, his words going straight from his lips to her heart.

Warmth filled Abigail. Warmth, and hope, and love, and all the good feelings she had spent so long being afraid of. She tangled her fingers in Jasper's hair, where the snow was already melting. He was naked from the shift, and his body was hard against hers. The chill on his skin was fading, and she felt his heat even through all her winter layers. She was desperate for his touch.

And sad. So desperately, heartbreakingly sad for her wonderful Jasper, who loved Christmas and loved her and was about to lose half of his soul.

And there was nothing she could do to help him. She'd leapt off the cliff and now they were both falling.

But not alone. Together. She'd reached out for his hand and he'd taken it, just as she had taken his.

Because he'd been afraid she would run away when she found out what he was. And now? Was he still afraid, that she would leave him alone in his time of absolute need? She wouldn't blame him if he was. He knew how brittle she was, and she had already run driven him away once.

She slid her hands up Jasper's chest. His heart beat like thunder under her palms.

"I have something for you," she told him, her heart in her throat.

One final Christmassy olive branch. Not much. Not enough. But a small symbol for her Christmas-loving dragon, something to show him she had come to give him her heart, even before she knew he was a shifter. And that she would still stay, now, with the human Jasper. No matter what.

She darted over to the coat rack and rummaged in her dripping jacket's pocket. It had to still be here— yes! Soaking wet and the Christmas wrap was starting to disintegrate, but still in one piece.

Abigail turned to Jasper, holding out her gift. "Merry Christmas," she said quietly, trying to keep the tears from her eyes.

18

JASPER

Jasper stared at the small parcel his mate was holding out to him. *His Abigail*, he corrected himself. *No.* His *mate*. Even if he was no longer a dragon, she would always be his mate.

She had brought him a present. A *Christmas* present. For him. For who she had thought he was— just an ordinary man with a strange Christmas obsession.

She couldn't have known what it meant. Bliss swept through him, human and dragon. A Christmas gift from his mate… if this had to be his last night as a shifter, at least his dragon would disappear suffused with the joy of receiving a gift.

He took the parcel from Abigail's hands with reverent tenderness. "Thank you," he breathed, and she smiled nervously.

"I hope you like it," she said, ducking her head.

"I already love it," he reassured her. It was wrapped in paper and bubble-wrap. The paper was already disintegrating and fell away at his touch, but he had to wrestle a bit with the bubble-wrap. He could only see glimpses of what was hidden beneath it. Glints of red and orange— something hard, with smooth, rounded edges— and—

He ripped through the bubble-wrap and his fingers stuttered as though electrified. *Gold.*

The plastic fell away. His gift was a stone heart, inlaid with gold. A jasper heart, all the colors of his dragon held in a polished gem the size of Abigail's fist. The front of the heart was rounded and smooth, showing off the swirls and whorls of the stone.

He turned it over. His fingers hadn't lied: the flat back of the stone heart was inlaid with gold. The mineral sang to his heart and his dragon sang back, crooning deep inside him. Jasper ran his thumb over the gold decoration. Scrolls ran around the edge of the heart, and in the middle—

He closed his eyes. There was no way Abigail could have had this custom inscribed only this morning, but that didn't matter. She had bought it for him. Her love for him infused every atom of it, every particle of jasper and gold, shining from the inscription:

Merry Christmas, to the one who has my heart.

He closed his hand over the jasper heart. Gold sang against his skin, and his own heart sang inside his chest.

"I know it's cheesy…" Abigail began. He didn't let her get any further. Heart singing, he pulled her into his arms, kissing her until she melted against him.

He still had the stone heart in his hand, pressed against the curve of her lower back. The gold sang against his skin— and inside him, through him, into his mate, his Abigail, until the air around them seemed to shimmer with it.

Jasper broke the kiss. He looked down at his mate— and blinked. *I have to be imagining this.*

The air *was* shimmering. Lights flickered through the air around him and Abigail, like a thousand fireflies or a thousand tiny suns. Abigail's eyes were wide.

"Are you seeing this?" she breathed.

"Yes."

"Is it a dragon thing?"

"I don't know," Jasper admitted. It was magic. It had to be magic. But what sort of magic? What was it for?

He pulled Abigail closer. Everywhere she touched him, his skin was on fire. It was as though the lights weren't just around them, they were inside him, as well, flooding his veins. He looked down at Abigail. Was it just a reflection, or were there lights in the depths of her eyes, as well?

The lights grew brighter, and the song of the gold became louder, chiming like bells in his ears. In his heart. His *soul.*

And then he knew.

"Abigail," he whispered, and her gaze locked on to his. "We don't need to go to my hoard. It isn't up in the mountains. Not anymore." He drew his hand around from her back and raised it. "It's right here."

The heart was glowing, the gold gleaming bright as the heart of a fire. *His* gold, the first gold gifted to him by his mate. The heart of his hoard.

He folded Abigail's hands over it and felt the shiver that went through her as she felt its power.

"Abigail George. Will you be my mate, mine to protect and care for, as long as we both live?"

"I will," Abigail said at once, her face alight with happiness. "Will you be mine? To protect and care for, as long as we both live?"

He didn't know if that was the proper way to do things, his human mate offering him her protection. But he didn't hesitate. "I will." Proper or not, it was right. After all, hadn't she protected and cared for him today?

He led her through to the bedroom, and the bed he hadn't slept in since he arrived in Pine Valley. It was huge, a heavy, super-king-sized four-poster piled high with comforters and pillows. Too huge for one person. Perfect for two. Perfect for his mate.

He laid the heart on the middle pillow, where it glowed, and turned to Abigail. He knew he was smiling like an idiot. He couldn't help it. Abigail smiled back, and reached up to touch his cheek.

"I love you," she said, and laughed. "Warning you now. Now that I've started saying it, I don't think I'll be able to stop."

"Good." He unzipped her snow jacket. *His* snow jacket, which hid her curves like a tent. She shimmied it the rest of the way off.

"I love you," she said again, eyes bright.

He stripped off his own jacket, and then started on her sweater.

"I love you!"

Shirt. Pants. Garments began to litter the floor.

"I love you. I— oh!"

Jasper shed his underwear and clasped her to him, skin to skin. Her fingers tightened on his shoulders and her eyes bloomed dark with desire. "I love you," she repeated, her voice rough. "I love you, I love you, I… ohhh…"

Her skin was so soft. He wanted to touch every inch of her, caress her, stroke her and nuzzle her and kiss her, but every brush of her body against his made his need more urgent. He was breathless with it, so hard he ached.

This was different to the other times they had slept together. More primal. Before, he had lain with her. Tonight, he would claim her.

He met her eyes and found the same wild, passionate desire in them that burned in him like wildfire.

"I feel—" Her eyes widened, lips parted as though she was tasting the air. Tasting the magic and desire that filled the world around them. "Oh, God, Jasper. Take me. Make me yours!"

He pushed her back onto the bed, gently but firmly. Her skin was creamy against the richly colored comforters. Her whole body quivered under him, her breasts heavy and inviting, the scent of her arousal intoxicating his senses.

Jasper kissed her breasts, one after the other, sucking her nipples into his mouth and making circles around them with his tongue until Abigail's whole body was shaking with small tremors of desire. He lifted his head and looked up at her.

She stared back, cheeks pink, eyes black and bright with need. She ran her fingertips down his back, digging in with her nails. "Please," she begged.

He rose up above her, pulling her arms from around himself and kissing the palms of her hands. he nipped the tip of one finger and she groaned. He nipped another and then pinned her wrists above her head.

Abigail lay stretched out beneath him, vulnerable and beautiful and *his*. She was giving herself to him, fully and forever. His mate. His Abigail.

"I love you," he whispered, and thrust into her.

19
ABIGAIL

Abigail cried out as Jasper entered her. He was so hard and hot and so, so perfect. Pleasure built inside her, so strong already she almost came as he buried himself fully inside her.

Her whole body felt as though it was about to fly apart. Was this magic? The lights had followed her from the front room— they danced around her, and inside her, too, she was sure. In her blood. Her heart.

She stared up into Jasper's ember-bright eyes. The lights were there, as well. And the gold…

Jasper was pinning her wrists with one hand. Still buried deep inside her, he reached up for something on the pillow above her head. Then he pressed something into her hands. The jasper heart.

She still blushed when she remembered the inscription. It was so cheesy, so ridiculous. So true. Jasper had her heart. He had stripped away her spiky walls and all her fearful defenses, and her heart was his. Forever.

Jasper closed both his hands over hers, trapping the heart between their palms. His dark hair fell over his face. With his burning eyes, he looked somehow more than human. More primal and powerful.

She shivered with anticipation— and then something else.

Jasper leaned down, whispering in her ear, "Do you feel it?"

Something was ghosting over her skin, tracing feather-light trails down her wrists and arms. She looked up. "The gold?"

Gold was flowing from the heart, shining tendrils winding like metal ribbons down her arms. Several tendrils looped around her wrists, and others kept moving down her body. She twitched as they tickled over her ribs and Jasper groaned, thrusting against her hips. Her head fell back, pleasure pulsing through her as his cock pressed against her most sensitive places, so overwhelmed she barely noticed where the other gold went.

Then it tightened around her ankles, pulling her legs apart.

She looked up at Jasper, shocked. She had already opened her legs for him, but this was different; the gold was spreading them further apart, transfixing her beneath him.

Gold at her wrists, gold at her ankles. The tendrils were slender— there hadn't been much gold on the heart, after all— but she knew that if she tested her bonds, they would not break. Her heart fluttered.

Jasper pulled out of her. "Is this alright?" he asked, his voice rough.

His eyes were darker than she had ever seen them, the pupils so large there was only the barest hint of gold and red around the edges. His hair fell over his face, tangled and wild. His skin was flushed. Muscles bunched in his shoulders and biceps. His whole body was like a bow pulled tight, powerful and strong.

She couldn't move. That didn't matter. She didn't want to move. She wanted him, here, now. Forever. Hers.

"Make me yours," she replied, her own voice throaty with passion. Jasper groaned out loud and thrust into her. Harder than before. Primal. *Perfect.*

He pounded into her so hard it left her breathless, then thrust in again, until she had no breath left even to moan. Desire built inside her, every thrust stoking the bonfire of her love until she thought her whole body would catch fire. She was completely open beneath him, helpless and vulnerable and lost in passion.

She gasped and cried out, toes curling, and then opened her eyes to find herself caught in Jasper's gaze. His eyes were like coals, black with heat. His fingers tightened around her own. The stone heart seemed to pulse between their palms, and the gold burned on her wrists and ankles.

"My mate," Jasper gasped. Abigail's breath caught in her throat. "My own. Forever. Always. My mate, my Abigail…"

His voice was low and hitching, as though he could barely control it. Barely control himself. Abigail flexed underneath him. She was trapped by the gold but she could still move her hips, her body, returning his thrusts with the same frenzied passion until—

Abigail cried out wordlessly as pleasure overtook her. Stars burst in front of her eyes. Real, or magic? She didn't know. She didn't care. She was dissolving, floating in an endless ocean of stars, strange constellations stretching out on all sides. She *was* the stars, burning and shining and so alive with happiness she thought she might cry.

She opened her eyes. Her vision was hazy; she blinked, found Jasper's face, drowned herself in his gaze. His ember eyes. Her dragon.

She raised her head, demanding a kiss. When he kissed her, she bit down on his lip until he gasped, then softened, teasing his hips until he groaned. The noise reverberated against her lips, deep into her bones. She could no longer tell where her body ended, and his began. They were together, bound by love, floating in a velvet sky of stars.

"Mine," she gasped. Pleasure was still cascading through her, new waves shuddering through her body with Jasper's every thrust. "My mate."

Jasper cried out, thrusting deeper and harder into her as he came. The chains around her wrists and ankles tightened— and then released, and he was in her arms, falling beside her in the bed, limbs tangling together and lips locked in a kiss she hoped would never end.

They lay still together, lost in wonder and happiness. Jasper's eyes were embers again, dancing like firelight as he kissed her. Slow kisses. Leisurely. Endless.

Abigail smiled and stretched, pressing her body against his as he slowly trailed kisses down her neck. She shivered as he reached her collarbone. She was sated, exhausted— but these kisses might convince her otherwise…

Then he reached her breastbone, and she jerked. "I feel it!"

Jasper was up on his elbows in a second, eyes furrowed with concern. "What?"

"The— the—" It was too wonderful. She couldn't put it into words. She pressed her hand against his chest, hoping he would understand.

His eyes widened. "The mate bond? You feel it, too?"

Abigail nodded. There it was, in her heart. In the space that she now realized had always been waiting for it. A warmth, a light, like a sun inside her chest—and a glowing chain that linked her to Jasper. If she concentrated, she could feel it. If she closed her eyes…

She could *see* it, stretching between their bodies. Glowing gold-bright, like the gold that had bound her during the ritual. Connecting her to him, and him to her. Forever.

She smiled. "Too late for me to run away now."

Jasper narrowed his eyes mischievously. "Too late indeed." He buried his hands in her hair. "I guess I'm stuck with you."

"And I'm stuck with you, dragon-man."

"*Your* dragon-man."

"Mine." She liked that. God, how she liked that. "My Jasper. My mate."

Desire kindled in his eyes and Abigail laughed. "My mate," Jasper echoed back at her. "Say it again."

"Mine." Jasper's eyes burned brighter, and she knew she was playing with fire. Excitement flared inside her. "My mate. My— Jasper!"

20

JASPER

25 DECEMBER

CHRISTMAS DAY

"Thank God for interfering older sisters," Jasper muttered, pulling a bag of coffee from the cupboard. Even though he'd barely spent more than a few hours in the cottage over the last week, Opal had kept the pantry fully stocked. Even the milk was fresh. Left to his own devices, Jasper knew, he would have been dining on stale bread and water.

No longer, though. Not with his mate here. He knew what she liked; he was already planning how to re-stock the pantry when the shops opened after the holiday. All of Abigail's favorites. And some of his own. He was sure he would be able to win her over to them.

After all, he'd won her over to Christmas.

He glanced over his shoulder at Abigail. She was lying stretched out on the sofa in front of the fire in the front room. They'd barely been out of each other's arms since the afternoon before, let alone out of sight. Except for certain vital, private functions, of course.

Jasper turned back to the counter and tipped coffee into the French press. A moment later, the soft patter of bare feet on floorboards warned him of Abigail's approach.

She wrapped her arms around him from behind.

"Couldn't stay away?"

"Mmmm." Abigail held him tighter, pressing her breasts against his back. "Maybe. Congratulations, you're more interesting than the sofa."

"And I'm glad to hear it." He twisted around and kissed the top of her head. "Coffee's almost ready. How are you feeling?"

Abigail released him and walked around to lean against the counter. Jasper's heart glowed as he looked at her. Though, really, it had hardly stopped glowing since he claimed her.

She was wearing a pair of his trousers, the hems rolled up around her ankles, and another of his shirts. The soft cotton hung over her curves like the garment was made for her.

"You look beautiful," he told her, and she wrinkled her nose. "I told you, you don't need to be embarrassed. Everyone's going to know—"

"*Oh God,*" Abigail groaned, and Jasper laughed as she covered her face.

"Everyone's going to know that you're my mate. Trust me, you having to borrow my clothes is by far the least embarrassing way the Heartwells have been introduced to a new member of the family." He poured the coffee and added a generous dollop of cream to both cups. "After Cole's gone to sleep, maybe I'll convince Opal to reveal the torrid story of how she and Hank met…"

"Opal's your sister, right? And Hank's your brother-in-law." Abigail paused, a line forming between her eyebrows. "And Cole is… four?"

"And very big on jumping on people from roofs." Jasper held her coffee out of reach until she kissed him, grumbling. "Speaking of which, I recommend hiding behind me at all times when we're outside."

"I think I can survive a four-year-old jumping on me," Abigail retorted, blowing on her coffee to cool it. Jasper watched her lips, hypnotized. When she started to sip, he groaned aloud— making sure she could hear him.

A vivid blush spread across her cheeks. "*Stop* it. We're going to see your family in twenty minutes." She shot a glance out the window, into the pre-dawn darkness. Then her eyes crept back to Jasper. When she saw that he was still watching her, her blush burned even more fiercely. "*Hey.*"

She was frowning, but a pleased smile pulled at the corners of her mouth as she sipped more coffee. Jasper leaned back against the counter, preening. He raised his hands in surrender, and started on his own coffee.

Abigail's eyes flicked over to him again, and he laughed out loud. "I shouldn't have teased you. You're right, we don't have time. If we're late, we'll have a hundred pounds of juvenile dragon rage to deal with."

"A hundred pounds? What sort of four-year-old weighs ninety pounds?" Abigail's eyes widened. "Oh. Of course. You're pretty massive as a dragon, so Cole…"

"…Is the size of a small pony, yes." He waited for Abigail to work through this new fact. She grimaced, and then grinned at him.

"Maybe I'll hide behind you after all," she relented. She finished her coffee and licked her lips in a way that made Jasper wish they really did have more than twenty minutes before they were meant to meet his family. "We'd better get moving if we're going to dig my car out…"

"We don't need a car."

She snorted. "I'm not *walking*— oh. Oh. That isn't the only option, is it?" She put down her cup, wonder dawning on her face. Jasper's heart glowed as he watched her, and he stopped resisting the impulse to pull her into his arms. She buried her face in his chest and groaned. "There's so much I'm going to need to get used to, isn't there?"

"Absolutely." He kissed the top of her head.

"Will your wings be okay? Yesterday—"

"I told you, I'm a fast healer." He straightened his shoulders, striking as heroic a pose as he could manage while still clasping Abigail to his chest. "Didn't you check *all* my cuts and bruises already? I seem to remember you making a very detailed survey…"

"Mmm." Abigail bent her head back and narrowed her eyes. She traced the mark on his lip with one gentle finger. "So, what? You're keeping this one deliberately?"

Jasper caught her hand before she could pull it away. Her touch was too sweet to lose. Especially there.

The cut on his lip was almost healed— but unlike his other wounds, this one was leaving a scar. This had never happened to him before. He wasn't doing it on purpose, no matter what Abigail believed.

But he knew what it was. He knew *why* it was, why of all the scrapes he had gotten himself into over the years, this would be the only one to leave a permanent mark. Because that scar on his upper lip was where Abigail had pulled a splinter from his dragon's jaw, bringing his human side back from the edge.

It was a memory. A precious, beautiful memory, and one he was proud to keep on his skin.

"Every time I look in the mirror, I'll remember what you did for me," he said softly. Abigail's eyes flicked to his, suddenly dead serious. "You saved me. First in the forest, and then when you brought me the new heart of my hoard— I didn't even know that was possible. You showed me a magic I never knew could exist." Abigail's eyes filled with tears as he kissed the tips of her fingers. He waited until she had blinked her eyes dry before he continued: "Plus, I think it makes me look *very* dashing."

"Oh, you— *guh!*" Abigail knocked her forehead against his chest, half-laughing, half-sniffing. "I *knew* you were doing it on purpose."

"Maybe," Jasper teased her. He bent his head against hers and inhaled, breathing in his mate's scent. She was all soft curves in his arms, but he knew that even without her spiky armor, those curves hid a spine of pure steel. His to protect— and she would protect him, in return. His scar was a reminder of that, too.

He glanced up at the clock. His human side grated at having to let go of her, even briefly— but his dragon wanted to show off to Abigail, too. And now was its chance.

"Ready to go?" he asked, and Abigail's eyes shone into his.

"Yes," she said.

21

ABIGAIL

"First things first," Jasper said, calling back over his shoulder as he darted back into the bedroom, "I'll need you to carry these."

He came back in carrying two massive sacks over one shoulder. Abigail gaped.

"You're kidding! I won't be able to carry those *and* hold on!" She was still trying to comprehend the idea that they were going to be *flying* up to the Heartwell lodge. That was more than enough for her brain right now, even with the coffee. Add two massive sacks of presents, and the only direction she would be flying was going to be straight down.

Jasper frowned. "No, not those. I'll carry the presents. I need you to carry *these*."

He held out the bundle he had been holding under his other arm. Abigail took it. "Clothes?" It made sense; he seemed to always be naked when he shifted from dragon to human. But, still…

"You didn't think I was going to spend Christmas dressed like this, did you?" Jasper spread his arms and paraded himself across the kitchen floor, almost knocking the coffee pot off the counter with one of the sacks as he spun in a circle.

She looked him up and down, since that was clearly what he was after. He was wearing a navy sweater and dark pants. "Ah," she said, unwrapping the bundle slightly. "Not Christmassy enough?"

Something glittered deep in the bundle of clothing. A warning gleam of tinsel and Christmas red, green and white.

Abigail met Jasper's eye and grinned wickedly. "You're trusting me not to throw this into a snowdrift in disgust while your back is turned?"

Jasper's eyes sparkled. "You'll have to decide which is worse: me wearing those for Christmas brunch, or me wearing nothing at all."

Abigail pulled the sweater free and held it up. "Oh, God," she muttered. "You know, that's actually going to be a difficult decision."

But it wasn't. Her heart felt light. A few days ago, even the sight of the Christmas sweater would have made her flinch, but today the only thing it hurt was her sense of fashion. And for Jasper, she was willing to let that slide. Horrific as the Christmas sweater was, she stuffed it into a backpack with the rest of Jasper's change of clothes.

"Now…" Jasper smiled at her, eyes glittering. Her stomach flipped over. She still couldn't believe— no, that wasn't right. With everything she had seen in the last twenty-four hours, she absolutely believed in magic. In shifters. In a gorgeous, caring, sweet man who could turn into a powerful dragon.

And, looking into his eyes, she knew he loved her. And she loved him back.

"Ready?" he asked, opening the front door. The world beyond was pure white, snow drifts piled up over the road and trees.

Abigail hugged the bundle of clothes to her chest. "Ready," she replied, unable to keep the grin off her face.

Jasper threw the sacks into a snowdrift and leapt outside. One step, two, and he had stripped off his shirt and pants. He spread his arms, bare skin goose-bumping in the chilly air, and then *changed.*

Abigail stared, entranced. Scales shimmered under Jasper's skin, and then his whole body shone with strange, magical light. Wings burst out of his shoulders and the light became brighter, almost blinding. Abigail shaded her eyes. She could see movement inside the light, Jasper's body shifting its shape, becoming bigger.

Then the light faded, and a dragon was staring down at her with ember-bright eyes.

Abigail reached out. Jasper lowered his head, and she stroked him between his eyes, marveling at how smooth his scales were. He was right; his dragon was completely healed. Except for one scar on his top lip.

She touched it gently, and then looked deep into the dragon's eyes. Jasper was magnificent. even the scar didn't mar his dragon's powerful beauty.

Jasper knelt down, so graceful it was like a courtly bow. Abigail took a deep breath.

This is it. I'm going to fly on a dragon.

Jasper had two lines of hard ridges running from his snout, up over his eyes and down his spine. She grabbed hold of the nearest one and pulled herself up just in front of his wings, where the two lines of ridges separated, leaving a broad space where she could sit and hold on.

Abigail settled herself as firmly as she could. Her heart was beating so fast, it felt like it was about to explode.

Jasper reached one clawed foreleg into the snowdrift to retrieve the sacks of presents and then swung his massive head around, a question in his burning eyes.

"Yes," Abigail replied at once. "Let's go!"

Jasper spread his wings, beat them twice with a noise like thunder, and leapt into the air. Cold wind whipped past Abigail's face, but she was dressed warmly— and besides, she was too amazed to notice it.

The world dropped away as the dragon flew higher and higher, as graceful as a bird in the air. Mountains tipped and tilted as he changed direction and Abigail held on tight, but never felt unsafe. She knew her dragon would never let her fall.

She was flying. She was really, truly, *flying.*

Abigail let out a whoop of pure joy, then laughed as Jasper roared. The sound reverberated through her, making her blood fizz. They rose higher and higher above the mountains as dawn broke over the horizon.

Abigail closed her eyes. Memories were stirring inside her. What was this like? She felt the icy wind on her face and laughed, remembering. It was like when Jasper had taken her ice-skating. She had been scared at first, but Jasper had shown her she could trust him. He'd covered her eyes and guided her across the ice and it had almost felt like flying…

Abigail opened her eyes and gasped. The sky was a thousand shades of lavender and pink, and Jasper's scales were reflecting the dawn light, shimmering like liquid gold. She had never seen anything more beautiful.

Jasper made a soft noise. Abigail followed the direction he was pointing his head, and saw the Heartwell lodge far below them. Jasper tilted his wings, wheeling slowly down towards the building.

Anxiety gnawed at Abigail's insides, just for a moment. She didn't want this magical flight to end. Then she saw something that filled her with wonder.

More dragons were flying up from the grounds around the lodge. One, two— three, the third tiny compared to the others, jet-black and rocketing straight towards Jasper and her.

"Jasper, look!" she cried out, but he had already seen them. He flared his wings out, hovering in the air as the tiny dragon swooped around him like a crazed missile.

Abigail laughed out loud, watching the child dragon play in the air. *That must be Cole!* she thought. His scales were a gleaming jet black, and his eyes were midnight blue. The bigger dragons glided up behind him, graceful and serene, but he was beating his wings as frantically as a hummingbird.

They must be Jasper's sister and brother-in-law, Abigail thought, looking at the other dragons. One was silvery-white, but as the light caught its scales, it revealed other colors: pinks, greens, lavenders. The other dragon's scales were a bold forest-green.

Abigail looked down at Jasper again, and his burnished, red-orange scales. She hid a grin. It's a good thing I changed my mind about Christmas, she told herself. Jasper isn't the only Christmas dragon in his family – together, they're all the colors of the season, red, green and white!

Jasper's family flew either side of him as they all returned to the snowy ground. Jasper peeled away at the last moment and landed behind the lodge.

Abigail slipped off his back and turned around just in time to see him shift. The magical light of his transformation had barely faded before he swept her into his arms.

He was completely, gloriously naked. Abigail ran her hands down his back, enjoying the feel of his lean muscles under her palms. He made a rough sound in the back of his throat and pulled her closer.

"Cold?" she teased.

"Mmm." Jasper nipped her lower lip. "I— oh, damn." His gaze became distant. "Cole's on the hunt. Where are my clothes?"

Abigail thrust the bundle into his hands, laughing. He dressed with frantic speed, hopping on one leg in the snow to pull on his trousers. Abigail stuffed her fist against her mouth, stifling an attack of unstoppable giggles as her mighty, powerful dragon got his head stuck in his shirt.

"Here, let me help—" She pulled the shirt straight and kissed him. Jasper's hair was even more unruly than usual and she ran her fingers through it, drawing him close.

"Darling," he murmured against her lips. "Look out!"

He picked her up and swung around as a black shadow charged at them from around the side of the house. Cushioned in his arms, Abigail barely felt the impact as the black dragonling launched itself onto

Jasper's back. For a moment, Jasper managed to carry the weight of them both; then they all fell in a pile into the snow.

"Cole!" Abigail heard Jasper's exasperated shout, and then his laughter as the little dragon flapped snow into the air. Claws scrabbled against Abigail's heavy jacket as Cole tried to turn himself right-side-up. He almost managed it, and then all three of them lost their balance again.

They rolled in a tangle of limbs and wings and suddenly there was a flash and instead of a jet-black dragon there was an adorable four-year-old boy snuggling up between Abigail and Jasper. He had a shock of black hair, and bright, mischievous eyes.

She blinked down at him. "Hello!"

The little boy blinked back, suddenly shy. "'Lo," he whispered, and flung his arms around Jasper, who laughed.

"Cole, don't be silly! This is Abigail. She's going to be your aunt."

Abigail met his eyes in shock, but the love in his gaze washed away her surprise. She wrinkled her nose at him. "Aren't you meant to ask me, first?"

Jasper's eyes widened. "I— oh, God. I didn't, did I? I never actually asked you to marry me." He reached over Cole to grasp her hand. "Abigail, will you—"

"Jas!"

A dark-haired woman ran around the side of the house, closely followed by a red-haired mountain of a man. Jasper groaned. Little Cole looked from his uncle, to Abigail, and back, a curious expression on his face.

Abigail felt another giggle building up inside of her.

The woman stopped beside them, panting slightly. She greeted Abigail with a broad smile. "Jas, is this— ?"

"Right!" Jasper announced. He stood up with one arm around Abigail and Cole slung under the other. "Opal— dearest of sisters— please take your offspring…"

He handed Cole off to Opal, and then turned back to Abigail, capturing her waist with both hands. "Abigail," he said, his voice rough. "No— wait…"

He knelt down in the snow, staring up at her with eyes that burned with love. "Abigail, will you marry me?"

Abigail's breath caught in her throat. To her horror, tears filled her eyes— and Jasper saw. A look of terrified consternation flashed over his face. He began to stand up.

Abigail put her hands on his shoulders, forcing him to stay on his knees until she could say the words burning in her heart: "Yes, yes! Of course I'll marry you, Jasper. Yes. How could I say anything else?"

She flung her arms around his neck as he stood up. "I love so you much."

Then he was kissing her, and all her words, all the rest of the world, melted away. There was only Jasper's soft lips against hers, his arms around her—and the magic that connected them.

She could still feel it, that mysterious gold-bright chain that bound them together. His heart to her heart, her soul to his soul. And now they were going to be married. She was happy in so many ways she had never dared to hope for.

Jasper kissed her again, hard, and then released her, letting his hands slide down her arms until he was holding both her hands. He looked over her shoulder, and then turned her to face his family.

"Abigail, I'd like you to meet my sister Opal, and her husband Hank. And you've already met this tiny menace, Cole." He squeezed Abigail's hands. "Everyone… this is Abigail. My mate and, soon, my wife."

Abigail bit down on her lower lip. She was so happy, she thought if she let herself say anything, she would burst into happy tears. Opal came up and hugged her.

"Welcome to the family, Abigail." She shot Jasper a sharp life. "*Wife?* I don't see a ring on her finger, Jas. I thought you would have given her the pick of your hoard."

"About that…" Jasper released one of Abigail's hands and reached into his trouser pocket. His eyes smoldered into hers. When he pulled his hand out, he was holding the jasper heart she had given him. "Abigail, my love. Ignore my sister. I'm not going to give you just any old ring."

Gold began to flow from the stone, curling through the air like ink in water. Jasper raised Abigail's left hand. "You deserve no less than the heart of my hoard," he said, and the gold flew onto her finger, twisting and turning into a perfect gold ring.

Abigail gasped as she lifted her hand to look closer. What looked like a pattern running around the outside of the ring was really a dragon. And not just any dragon. *Her* dragon.

"Jasper," she whispered. "It's beautiful."

"It's yours," he said simply. "And so am I. Forever."

Her heart swelled with more emotion than her body could contain. She took a shaky breath, still not trusting herself to speak, and looked deep into Jasper's eyes. Did he know how overwhelming this was for her? After so many years without love, to feel so much of it, so quickly… she was drowning.

"I understand," Jasper whispered, kissing her ring-finger.

And suddenly she wasn't drowning; her body still wasn't big enough to contain everything she was feeling, but that didn't matter, because the invisible golden chain that connected her to her mate was acting as a river between them. Love flowed through it, his to her, and hers to him. She wasn't drowning in it— she was flying, and it was so perfect she almost cried.

She felt a hand on her shoulder. Opal pulled her into a hug, then looked into her face hard. Abigail blinked. Had she started crying? God, she hoped not. The first time she met Jasper's family. God, how embarrassing. She leaned back against Jasper, her knees shaking. Maybe she was flying, but she wasn't very good at it yet.

"Sweetheart, you look exhausted." Opal glared at Jasper. "Have you even fed her this morning?"

"Just coffee—" Jasper began. Guilt flashed through his eyes, too late to ward off his sister's wrath.

Opal rolled her eyes. "Do I have to do *everything?* Come on. Time for breakfast."

She marched off, snapping her fingers at the rest of them to follow her. Jasper ducked his head towards Abigail, concern in his eyes.

"I'm sorry— if this is all too much…"

Abigail laid her left hand against his cheek. Her ring shone in the morning light. "I'm fine. This is all wonderful."

He still looked worried. Abigail bit her bottom lip, concentrating. The golden chain that connected them, that acted like a river…

She sent her happiness through it, bright and sparkling and endless. Jasper's eyes flared, and he pulled her into a kiss that made their golden mate-bond sing.

"Uncle Ja-a-asper! Auntie Abigail!" Cole yelled from the lodge's front door. "Come in for breakfast!" Abigail turned in time to see him exchange a whispered conversation with Hank. "Dad says if you don't come now, I get to eat all of your food!"

"That sounds like a threat we should take seriously," Abigail said, laughing.

"Very." Jasper kissed her again, and then led him inside, where the others were waiting for them around a table piled high with food, and surrounded with laughter and Christmas cheer.

It was like no Christmas Abigail had ever experienced, and better than anything she could have imagined.

The Heartwell lodge was a beautiful building inside and out. Its huge, wood-paneled rooms with high rafters were all strung around with tinsel and lights, and Abigail strongly suspected it had been built deliberately with dragons in mind—when Cole shifted again and started climbing and flying around the rafters, she was sure of it.

Opal and Hank made her more than welcome, and by the time the breakfast dishes were put away she felt as though she had known them all for years. She held back when the family went through to the living room and started opening presents, until Cole ran up with a present in his hands.

"Do you want me to help you unwrap it?" she asked as the little boy wriggled onto the couch beside her.

"No, silly! It's for you!"

"What?" Abigail turned the present over and checked the tag. Her own name stared back at her. From— "Hank?"

Opal's broad-shouldered husband nodded at her. "Merry Christmas!"

"But how…?" Abigail met Jasper's loving gaze. "You planned this!"

"I always hoped you'd spend Christmas here. Ever since the moment I met you," Jasper said softly. "A *real* Christmas. With people who love you… and presents."

"Thank you." Abigail looked around the room, at Hank and Opal and Cole. "All of you. I never expected…"

"You're family now, Abigail," Opal said, snuggling into her husband's side. "Get used to it."

Abigail laughed. "I'll try. It might take a while."

"Take all the time you need," Jasper said magnanimously. "To start with, all the time it will take you to open all these presents…"

Paper piled up around Abigail as Cole helped her unwrap her gifts. Pretty things, and silly things, and all… for *her*.

"Thank you," she whispered to Jasper as Cole ran back to grab the next present from the pile under the tree.

"I know how much it means to you," he whispered back. "From now on, every Christmas will be like this." He reached under the tree and grabbed a soft-looking parcel. "This is for you, too. From me."

But you've already given me so much! Abigail caught the words before they reached her lips. She could already tell how important gift-giving was in this family, and would never hurt her mate by saying anything that sounded like rejecting a gift. She pulled the paper away and her eyes widened.

"It's a bit cheeky, I know…" Jasper leaned closer to her, wrapping one arm possessively around her waist. "I'm so glad it didn't end up in the garbage."

Abigail stroked the kitten plushie. She remembered stuffing it into her handbag before she left the apartment the day before. Jasper must have found it there. It still only had one eye and three legs, and its fur was sticking out in all directions, but her heart melted a little as she looked at it.

"I'm glad I didn't throw it out, either. It deserves another chance." A thought struck her, and she carefully balanced the toy in the Christmas tree, nestling it in between the other ornaments. "What do you think?"

"I think it looks very happy there," Jasper murmured, and kissed her.

22

JASPER

Jasper watched his mate. When she smiled, warmth blossomed in his heart. When she laughed at Cole's antics, his dragon grumbled in approval. When she looked at him…

Everything was right. Everything had come together. Him and his dragon— and their connection to Abigail, the glowing, golden chain that bound them together. His ring on her finger. Her love in his heart.

The day flew by. Breakfast, and then presents; lunch, and then the adults took turns dozing in front of the fire while Cole leapt on each of them in turn. Jasper manfully took Abigail's place in the being-jumped-on rotation; as he told her, whispering in her ear, he was the only person who was allowed to jump on her now.

She blushed, and every inch of his skin went hot with excitement.

He wanted to take her away somewhere private. Curl around her, warm her skin with his own, kiss her and caress her until they were both swept away on tides of pleasure.

Instead, he rolled into a defensive ball as Cole launched himself from the back of the sofa.

"Raar!"

"Raar yourself, you little menace!" Jasper unrolled and tackled Cole as he landed, tickling him mercilessly. Cole shrieked with laughter and wriggled in a way that was very familiar.

"Wait— *oop*." Jasper gasped as Cole shifted.

The little dragon blinked and stretched, clattering across the floor on clumsy claws to snuffle around the piles of wrapping paper and opened gifts. Jasper scoffed. He knew exactly what his nephew was after.

"You can't *possibly* still be hungry. No, don't eat those chocolates, you'll make yourself sick." He glanced over to the sofa where Opal and Hank were dozing, hoping for backup. No luck. They were either asleep, or pretending to be.

Groaning, Jasper crawled over to Cole and wrestled the box of chocolates off him. Cole whined, turning imploring midnight-colored eyes on him.

"That's not going to work on me," Jasper informed him, tapping him on his nose. "I'm not as soft-hearted as your mother."

Opal snorted from her position on the sofa. *Hah! Not asleep after all,* Jasper thought. But someone else was giggling, too.

Jasper looked over his shoulder to see Abigail grinning at him. She was lying on her front with her arms resting on the arm of the sofa, and her chin resting on her arms. The smile on her face was the most beautiful thing Jasper had ever seen.

Everything about her was the most beautiful thing Jasper had ever seen. Vaguely aware that something distinctly Cole-shaped was sneaking the box of chocolates out of his hands, Jasper gazed at his mate. He could have spent all day just looking at her.

Was this what it was like to have a mate? How did Opal and Hank ever get anything done?

Opal groaned, louder this time. "*Cole.*"

My stomach is bigger now! I'm hungry again!

"Then you can eat dinner, not my dark chocolate truffles." Opal climbed off the sofa, using her slumbering husband as leverage. She glanced out the window. "It's going to start getting dark soon—everything's ready to go, right, hon?"

She prodded Hank, who mumbled, "Yep, all good to go."

Jasper grinned at Abigail. Almost dinnertime. In the Heartwell family, that was the best part of Christmas. At least, according to him. And he hoped Abigail would feel the same.

"Dinner?" Abigail gave him a 'have mercy!' look. "I'm still stuffed from lunch. I don't think I could eat another bite," she said.

"Come on." Jasper crawled up to her and kissed her, ignoring the juvenile dragon who was trying to clamber onto his back. "It's Christmas. Stuffing yourself silly is the whole point."

"Where are we going?"

Abigail's cheeks were flushed from their trek up the hill behind the lodge. Jasper couldn't help her; he kissed her, only eventually remembering that she had asked him a question.

"You'll see soon," he reassured her, tucking a stray curl back under her hat. "In fact… here we are!"

"A bonfire?"

"All ready for a home-cooked meal. Cooked on the best flames there are." Hank jogged up behind them, dragon-shaped Cole on his shoulders. "Dragon-flame. Right, Cole?"

Yeah!

Abigail put one hand on her stomach and huffed out a breath. "I guess that gives me a few more hours to digest," she muttered thankfully.

"Not at all." Jasper grinned impishly at her. "Oh, the spit will take a while to cook, but you're forgetting appetizers. And aperitifs. And…" He frowned. "apps?"

"That's just short for 'appetizers'." Abigail poked him in the ribs.

"Nibbles, then. Snacks. Canapes?"

Abigail groaned. "I'm going to *explode.*"

Jasper slipped one arm around her waist. "It's Christmas!"

She groaned again. "So you keep reminding me. Maybe this is the real reason I avoided Christmas for so many years. Death by delicious food."

He pulled her close. "Don't worry. We'll work off all the calories later."

Abigail giggled, blushing, but Jasper was deadly serious. He'd claimed her, and she was wearing his ring, but he still wanted to show her his full hoard. Make it clear that he would be able to provide for her, *forever.*

And claim her again. And again, and again, and…

"Hmm?" Someone was trying to get his attention.

Opal raised one eyebrow at him. "You want to do the honors, Jas?"

"Light the fire?" Jasper looked at his sister, and then glanced across at Hank and his nephew. "Why don't we let Cole have a go this year? I think he's big enough now."

Cole's eyes glowed. He roared with glee, and then wriggled all over, as though even roaring wasn't enough to express his feelings. With a flash of light, he shifted, and ran around waving his arms. "Yes!

Yes! I want to light the fire! Can I, Mom? Can I Dad? Please? Pleeeeease?"

"Won't he get cold?" Abigail whispered in Jasper's ear. He supposed she had a point. Cole was running around butt naked in the snow. If he'd been a human child, that would have been a problem.

"He's a dragon," he explained. "We run hot. And if he feels a bit chilly, he can always— aha, there he goes."

Cole had barely waited for his parents to give him permission before he shifted and leapt into the air, jet-black wings beating frantically. He swooped around the bonfire, assessing it with his sapphire eyes.

"You can do it," Jasper whispered, and saw Abigail look up at him out of the corner of his eye.

"You're really good with him," she murmured, and snuggled more closely against him.

He was about to respond when Cole reared back in the air and let out a brilliant stream of dragon-fire. The bonfire burst into flame.

Hank whooped, and Abigail started clapping. Cole hovered in the air for a moment, and then half-flew, half-flopped back onto the ground.

I did it! he shouted telepathically, leaping around with excitement. *I set it all on fire! All by myself!*

"You did awesome, Cole!" Jasper called out, his heart bursting with pride for his nephew. "Want to help me get dinner on?"

Of course he was going to cook, he thought, ignoring Opal's surprised eyebrows. He had to provide for his mate.

Besides, night was falling. It was going to get colder. The other dragons would shift and go flying while they waited for dinner to finish cooking, but the cook got to stay by the fire… and cuddle with anyone else who happened to be around. Especially a warm, curvy human, who would be in need of a dragon's warmth.

His plan worked perfectly.

Opal, Hank and Cole flew off into the night, and Abigail settled happily by his side, snuggling so close that Jasper was ready to give up on dinner altogether and whisk her away to his hoard that very second.

Except Opal would have his head. And it wouldn't be fair on Cole, to ruin his very first dragon-fire Christmas dinner. So, maybe not.

Besides. There were *some* benefits to just sitting by the fire with his mate as Christmas dinner cooked.

Such as seeing the firelight dancing over her face. Watching her smile. Winding his fingers through hers, and imagining them sliding over his skin…

Later— far, far too much later— the others returned, and the whole family feasted on spit-roast lamb and potatoes baked in the coals. Cole stayed in dragon form, and ate until his belly was swollen and round. Jasper translated his telepathic groans of food-happiness to Abigail until she got hiccups from giggling.

The moon was high in the sky by the time the bonfire started to die down. Cole was asleep in front of the fire, lying on his back having dreams that made his claws twitch. Opal and Hank were sitting together, staring contentedly into the fire. And Abigail…

Abigail was looking up at him with an expression that said she remembered exactly what he'd said about working off the calories from their Christmas dinner.

"Well," Hank announced, stretching, "Feels like it might be time for bed. Merry Christmas, everyone." He stood up, picking up a sleepily grumbling Opal in one arm as though she was as light as a feather. "Come on, menace." He reached down and scratched Cole's head, and the dragonling promptly shifted back into a sleepy four-year-old boy. "Hup, up you go."

He paused, dozing wife in one arm, sleeping son on the other shoulder. "You coming?" he asked Abigail and Jasper.

Jasper met Abigail's eyes.

"We'll follow in a bit," she told Hank, her cheeks warming.

Hank grinned. "Merry Christmas," he said, and hesitated. "Hang on," he muttered to himself, freeing one hand to pat down his pockets. "Sure I had it here somewhere… Here, Jas. This arrived for you."

He handed Jasper a slip of card and made his way back down to the lodge.

Jasper concentrated, waiting until his heightened shifter hearing told him that the others were back inside. Then he directed a slow, teasing smile down at the woman snuggled into his side.

She sighed happily and wrinkled her nose. "What's that he gave you?"

"A card." Jasper looked closer. "A *Christmas* card. This looks like…"

He was about to say, *This looks like one of the cards from the Puppy Express,* when Abigail went stiff beside him. When he looked down at her, she was biting her lip nervously.

"Oh, that's. Um. The card I wrote you," she explained in a small voice. "You don't need to look at it— it's kind of embarrassing…"

"In that case, I'm definitely going to read it!" Jasper grinned at Abigail until she groaned and wrinkled her nose, and then inspected the Christmas card in the firelight. The front of the card was a scene of the same lake where they had stopped on their sled ride, with a festive border and Merry Christmas message.

He turned it over.

"Is this…" He frowned, and Abigail groaned softly. "Us?"

He held out the card. Abigail had drawn on the back— two figures, arms outstretched. She had scribbled bits out, and gone over and over other bits, but he could still make out…

"It is us," he decided. "Ice-skating, right?"

"Yes," Abigail admitted, hiding her face in his shoulder. "Except I'm not very good at drawing, I kept getting it wrong…"

Jasper peered at the card. True, the smaller figure looked like she only had one leg, and the larger one had at least four waving arms, but… "I love it." He pointed. "Is that our breath, in the cold air?"

"Mm."

"It looks like dragon-fire. In fact, I think we both look like we're flying in this picture…" He tucked the card carefully into his jacket's inside pocket. He was going to have it framed and put up in pride of place at home, no matter what Abigail said. It was a treasure. But right now… He raised one eyebrow at her. "How about it?"

"How about what? Oh— flying?" Her eyes lit up. "I love it. It's— I don't think there are words for how incredible it is, being up there in the sky with you."

"Want to do it some more?"

Her eyes narrowed with suspicion. "We're not going to follow Opal and Hank 'in a bit' at all, are we?"

"Nope."

"Back to your cottage?"

"Not that, either." He let her hang a moment longer, and then ducked his head to nuzzle into her neck.

"There's no snowstorm tonight, so I thought I'd take you somewhere special."

Abigail's eyes flicked from him, to the smoldering remains on the bonfire, to the moonlit sky— and back to him. "This seems pretty special to me."

"I was thinking somewhere more… glittery."

"Glittery?" Abigail blinked, and Jasper relented.

"My hoard." He held her left hand, feeling his ring under her glove. "The rest of it, that is. I want you to see it."

Abigail's eyes were bright. "Will it be… like last night?" She bit her bottom lip and Jasper groaned aloud.

"God, I hope so," he said. Abigail grinned.

"Is it far?"

"Only a short flight away."

Pure, simple excitement joined the desire on Abigail's face. "Then what are we waiting for?"

23
ABIGAIL

Abigail whooped as Jasper landed on a patch of black rock on the side of a mountain. It had, as he'd said, only been a short flight. Short enough to leave her wanting more, but long enough to get her pulse pounding. And if Jasper meant what he said about his hoard…

Desire pooled inside her, warm and liquid.

Jasper shifted. Abigail offered him his clothes, and he took them— but didn't put them on. Grinning at her over his shoulder, he walked up to a huge rock set into the side of the mountain. It was the size of a door, black and featureless in the moonlight.

The moonlight shone on Jasper, too, caressing the strong muscles of his back and ass, outlining his shoulders and bicep as he raised one arm toward the huge stone.

He hesitated, looking back at Abigail. The moonlight made everything silvery, but his eyes still burned ember-bright, red and gold. Right now, they looked vulnerable.

"I've never brought anyone here before," he said, his voice hushed.

Abigail walked up to him and took his hands in hers. The mate-bond sang as Jasper ran his thumb over her ring. "Show me," she whispered. "I want to know everything about you."

He smiled, raised his hand again, and the mountain moved.

Tendrils of gold curled around the edges of the door-sized rock, like roots growing out from the heart of the mountain. They pushed the rock aside, revealing a dark cave.

"Ladies first," Jasper said. He squeezed Abigail's hand and she frowned.

His smile was wobbling. He kept licking his lips. And his eyes still looked wary.

"Jasper, I've already chosen you," she said, placing one hand on his chest. "I love you. I want to spend the rest of my life with you. You don't need to be nervous."

Jasper took a deep breath. "I know. I just…" He shut his eyes and winced. "You'll see."

He led her into the cave. It was even deeper than it looked, going deep into the mountain. She was worried about losing her footing in the darkness, but just as the last beam of moonlight faded, another light came to life. The cave walls were lined with fern-like tendrils of gold, and they were *glowing*.

Abigail looked closer. Not ferns; the gold made patterns like ice crystals on a window. "This is beautiful," she murmured.

"Ye-es," Jasper said, sounding uncertain. "*This* is beautiful."

Abigail narrowed her eyes at him. *Interesting,* she thought. In the magical gold-light, he wasn't looking nervous anymore. More… embarrassed?

What does a dragon have to be embarrassed about? she wondered.

Then they turned a corner, and she knew.

Abigail gasped. She couldn't help it. Jasper's hoard was incredible. A huge cavern, piled high with gold and jewels. Objects of unbelievable value… and all on a particular theme.

She turned to her mate, eyes wide. "Jasper…"

"I know." He winced. "It seemed like a good idea at the time. God, this is so embarrassing… it's so much worse than the sweater…"

He covered his face. Abigail couldn't help it. She burst out laughing, which only made him groan louder.

"Jasper, stop." She pulled his hands away from his face and gestured at the treasure-piles. "This is— this is *wonderful.* Don't be embarrassed."

"But they're…" Jasper grimaced. Abigail caressed his cheek.

"Wonderful. Beautiful. Jasper, how could I think they were anything else?"

Arm in arm with her mate, she surveyed his hoard. Gold and jewels. That was traditional, she knew.

But of course, Jasper wasn't a traditional dragon. He was a Christmas dragon.

She stared wide-eyed at piles of Christmas baubles of all sorts, balls and bells and filigree stars, all gleaming, pure gold. Chains that looked more like tinsel and streamers. Even…

Abigail knelt down. "Is this… Rudolph?" she said, picking up the golden figuring and holding it out to Jasper. "With a ruby nose?"

Jasper stared at her, looking utterly lost. "Yes," he admitted. "But… you're smiling." He hesitated. "Do you… like it?"

Abigail's smile stretched across her face. "Like it?" She spun around. Everything in the cavern was one hundred per cent, ridiculously, *wonderfully* Christmassy.

It was so, so Jasper.

"I love it," she told him, and fell backwards onto the nearest pile of gold.

She'd expected it to be like falling onto gravel, or a riverbed of loose stones; instead, it was like falling into clouds. The gold moved under and around her, cushioning her perfectly.

"Is this— ?" she began.

"More dragon magic?" Jasper advanced towards her, his eyes glowing with more than ember brightness. "Yes."

Desire shot through Abigail and she gasped. Jasper's eyes locked on to her mouth. Anticipation sharpening the warmth inside her to white hot, Abigail slowly licked her lips.

Jasper was on top of her in a heartbeat. His body covered hers completely. "Damn it," he groaned. "You know how much I love it when you do that."

Gold moved under Abigail. Out of the corners of her eyes, she could see tinsel-like strands stretching towards her.

"I do," she agreed, and licked her lips again.

Jasper's eyes flared gold and red. He captured her lips with his, flicking his tongue out to explore her mouth. She kissed him back just as passionately. Her tongue teased against his, questing, playing.

She had longed for him all day. Her first Heartwell Christmas had been one miracle after another—happiness, family, love. Her desire for her mate had grown with every hour of the day, a low, strong simmer that made her skin prickle.

She'd expected a slow, languorous lovemaking, like they had shared the last few hours of Christmas Eve, when their bodies were tired but their desire for one another far from exhausted.

She hadn't expected this. The fire, the urgency. Pure need, white-hot and shining gold. Beautiful. *Right.*

She dug her fingers into Jasper's hair, deepening the kiss. Her skin was on fire, desperate for his touch. Her clothes were too heavy, stifling— but he was wonderfully, gloriously bare.

Abigail ran her hands up and down her lover's chest, sliding them around to dig her fingertips into the muscles of his back. He was hot, and hard, and *wonderful.* And groaning against her lips, his own hands pulling at her coat and shirt, fumbling with her trousers.

At last they were lying skin to skin. Abigail could feel Jasper's heartbeat against her breasts, the swell of his chest with every breath he took. The mate-bond sang inside them both, gold-bright and perfect.

Jasper gazed down at her, his eyes hooded with lust. "My darling," he murmured. He interlaced his fingers around hers, holding her hands against the gold above her head. "You are my most precious treasure. Everything else here pales in comparison to you."

His eyes raked down her body. Everywhere his gaze fell, her skin prickled with anticipation.

Abigail inhaled slowly, breathing in her dragon's scent. Sweet and spice, and pure masculine power. She moaned with desire and Jasper bore down on her. Her whole body melted against him, soft against his masculine hardness. She was hot and wet and willing, and he—

His eyes glowed into hers. "My mate," he whispered, his voice hoarse. "I have already given you the heart of my hoard. Now the rest of it will be yours, as well."

Gold chains— tinsel— snaked around her wrists, pulling her arms tight. Abigail wriggled against her constraints, glorying in the feeling of being pinned beneath her mate. More gold wound around her ankles, spreading her legs. She gazed up at Jasper, lips parted, the desire coursing through her veins so strong her vision was hazy.

"Everything I have, I share with you." Jasper caressed her cheek, moving his hands down over her breasts, her stomach, until Abigail thought she would burst with need. "All for you. My greatest treasure."

The gold responded to his words. Abigail felt the change through the mate-bond. Before, Jasper's hoard had been *his*, the chains around her wrists and ankles a mark of his claim on her. Now, the gold sang inside her, as well. Every piece of it. Her blood rang with its golden chimes.

"Oh, Jasper," she gasped. "My dragon. My only, my strong, wonderful mate—"

The chains were hers, now, too, but they stayed where they were. She wanted them there. She wanted to give herself, every part of herself, to him. To her Jasper, her dragon. Her mate.

Now and forever.

Her ring sang on her finger. *The heard of the hoard.* She felt it in her own heart. And Jasper was on top of her, his cock pressing against her entrance, and she had never wanted anything more.

"Please," she gasped.

Jasper's eyes were dark with lust. He moved on top of her, excruciatingly slowly. Abigail trembled with frustration. Didn't he know she needed this? Didn't he feel her desire, like she felt his through the mate-bond, lust and love and wonder woven together until she could barely see straight?

She looked deep into his eyes. He knew. Oh, he knew.

And she knew just what to do. She bit down on her lower lip. Hard. So hard she mewled with pain.

Jasper bore down on her. She felt his hunger, his desire, flooding through the mate-bond. He crushed his muscular chest against her breasts. Claimed his lips with hers. And he thrust inside her, so tenderly she thought she might cry from the overload of sensation.

He stilled when he was completely inside her. His heartbeat met hers, their breath mingling in the cool cavern. The scent of sweet spices filled her lungs. Her body. Her soul.

They moved together. Each thrust, each breath, each heartbeat. The fire inside Abigail was still wild, still urgent and raging with need, but Jasper controlled her. The gold controlled her. And her desire built with every moment, to heights she had never believed possible.

Her hands clenched. Every sensation seared across her soul. She was the heart of Jasper's hoard and his loved pressed in on her, filled her every pore, buoyed her up like a star in the oceans of eternity. *My mate. My mate.* His heartbeat thudded in her ears and she knew, gazing into the depths of his eyes, that her heartbeat filled his.

Gold-red eyes filled her vision. Her world. Dark pupils, wide with lust, and the flame of hot embers around their edges.

"Oh God, Jasper— !" she gasped, and pleasure overwhelmed her.

Sensual ecstasy caught her like a leaf in floodwaters. Pleasure cascaded through her, time and time again, until her limbs thrashed and she cried out in helpless abandon. The gold held her firm under her mate, until he drove into her harder than ever before, crying out as he spilled himself inside her.

The chains retreated as they lay together, panting. Abigail was almost disappointed; she wanted them on her forever, to show that she was Jasper's, his own, his mate. Forever.

She wrapped her arms around him and the glimmer of gold caught her eye. The chains had retreated— but not all of them. Gold clung to her wrists, delicate filigree chains of snowflakes and stars.

"I'm yours," she said to Jasper. Love flowered inside her and she sent it to him through the mate-bond as joy filled her veins. "See?"

Jasper touched the bracelets. "Mine," he whispered. His eyes smouldered into hers.

"Merry Christmas, Jasper," Abigail said, curling her body around his. He wrapped his arms around her, and she felt safer and more loved than she ever had in her life.

"Merry Christmas, my love," he said, and Abigail kissed him. He was right. This was the happiest Christmas she had ever known.

EPILOGUE
ABIGAIL

ONE YEAR LATER

The secret woke Abigail early. She'd felt it, these last few days, a *newness*, a strange new adventure growing inside her. But until now, she hadn't known what it was.

Wonder filled her. She allowed herself a private, amazed smile, letting joy flow through her veins as she stretched sleepily in her and Jasper's massive bed.

Love flowed back to her through the mate bond. Jasper had felt her wake up. She rolled over, ready to share her news.

And found the bed empty.

Abigail pushed herself up on her elbows, frowning. Where was he? This was Christmas morning— their second ever, the first since that wonderful first Christmas she had spent with her mate. Her *husband*. She looked at the rings on her finger. They had done things the wrong way around; her engagement ring was the plain gold ring Jasper had made for her last Christmas, with its inscribed dragon twining around her finger. The second was gold set with glittering jewels: one for each of the dates they had been on before Jasper claimed her as his own. One diamond for the terrible egg nog. One for the ice-skating, one for the dog-sledding. He'd even convinced her to include one for the night she almost lost him, their adventure up into Santa's belly.

And the biggest stone wasn't really for a date. It was for their first Christmas Eve together, and the moment they had chosen one another forever.

It was a jasper. Of course. Red and gold and almost as shining as her gorgeous husband's eyes.

Warmth blossomed inside her and she sent it down the mate bond. This wasn't as selfless as it sounded; as a human, she couldn't sense the mate bond with as much finesse as Jasper could. If he wanted to know where she was, all he had to do was think it. If she wanted to know where he was, she needed to flood the chain that connected them with overwhelming emotion.

Luckily, when it came to her and Jasper, that wasn't hard to come by.

Jasper was in the kitchen.

Any other morning, she could have forgiven him for that. But this morning, she had the secret. The best sort of news.

Abigail slipped out of bed, pulled on a silky dressing gown, and padded through to the kitchen.

Déjà vu caught her as she saw Jasper brewing coffee. They were in his cottage, of course. Just like last year. And they'd spent the previous night… well, *very* much like last year.

She crept up to Jasper on tip-toe, even though she knew she could never sneak up on him. He sighed with happiness as she wrapped her arms around him from behind.

"Awake already? I was going to surprise you with breakfast." Strangely enough, he didn't sound disappointed, especially after he turned around and snuck his hands under her silky robe. "But if you're awake…"

"Jasper, wait!" Abigail batted his hands away, laughing. He stopped at once, looking contrite.

"Of course. You need coffee first."

"I think *you're* going to need the coffee, actually." She smiled at his confused frown, and let him to the small kitchen table. "Sit down."

"All right…" Jasper's eyes narrowed. Abigail bit back a grin. He knew nothing was *wrong*; the mate bond would tell him if she was unhappy, or if the news she had for him was bad. But that was all he knew.

Much as she loved the magic that connected her to her mate, she was glad. She wanted to tell him herself.

Jasper sat down and she stood in front of him, feeling like her whole body was glowing with the secret.

"Sweetheart, what is it?"

"Something new. Or..." She took his hand and pressed it over her abdomen. "Some*one* new."

Jasper's eyes went wide. She felt his shock through the mate bond— and then his happiness, wild and pure and true. "Someone?"

Abigail held his happiness inside herself and then sent it back, overlaid with her own surprise and joy. "We're going to have a baby. Don't ask me how I know. When I woke up just now... it's like she had woken up, too, for the first time."

"She?" Jasper's eyes softened. "We're going to have a daughter?"

"A baby girl." Abigail laughed. She flung her arms around Jasper's neck and collapsed onto his lap, pressing herself against him. He stroked her belly. She knew she wasn't showing yet; it was too early for that. Too early for anything but the mate-bond magic to reveal her body's wonderful secret.

"I can *feel* her, Jasper. It's amazing. Like I can feel you."

Jasper bit his lower lip. A surge of warmth flowed through Abigail. He'd started doing that, this last year, and she knew he'd caught it from her. She felt the particular singing of the mate-bond inside her that meant her mate was focused entirely on her.

"I feel her, too," he whispered, his voice hushed with wonder. "Our daughter."

Happiness bubbled out of Abigail and she laughed out loud. "Oh, my darling," she cried out, pulling Jasper into a kiss.

"Merry Christmas, Jasper," she whispered. "Just think. Next year, she'll be here. Our first family Christmas."

She rested her forehead against his. A year ago, would she ever have imagined she could be this happy? But here she was, with everything she had never dared believe she truly wanted.

Every Christmas she was with Jasper, she found some new joy in life. She couldn't wait to discover what the next year brought them.

MORE PARANORMAL ROMANCE BY ZOE CHANT

A Mate for Christmas

A Mate for the Christmas Dragon
Christmas Hellhound
Christmas Pegasus
The Hellhound's UnChristmas Miracle
Christmas Griffin

A Gift for the Christmas Dragon (novella)

Shifter Suspense

Claimed by the Panther
Saved by the Billionaire Lion Shifter
Stealing the Snow Leopard's Heart
Craving the Kraken
Falling for the Shadow Dragon
Seducing the Soul-Eater

Hideaway Cove

The Griffin's Mate
The Sea Wolf's Mate
The Lightning Dragon's Mate
The Duskfire Dragon's Mate
The Kelpie's Mate

Standalone books not in series

Her Purr-fect Christmas Mate
Trusting the Tiger
Bear With Me

MONSTER ROMANCE BY MARIE CARDNO

The Monster Girlfriend series

How to Get a Girlfriend (When You're a Terrifying
Monster)
How to Get a Date with the Evil Queen
How to Get the Girl (And Not Destroy the World)

www.ingramcontent.com/pod-product-compliance
Lightning Source LLC
Chambersburg PA
CBHW020354120726
47904CB00002B/555